Kunu
Winnebago Boy Escapes

Kenneth
Thomasma

Jack
Brouwer
Illustrator

BAKER BOOK HOUSE
Grand Rapids, Michigan 49516

Grandview Publishing Company
Box 2863, Jackson, WY 83001

Second printing, September 1995

Library of Congress Cataloging-in-Publication Data

Thomasma, Kenneth.
    Kunu : Winnebago boy escapes
    183p.   cm. — (Amazing Indian children series)
    Summary: Following the forced removal of his people
from Minnesota to Crow Creek, South Dakota, a Winnebago
Indian boy embarks on a dangerous journey to return his
grandfather to his Minnesota homeland.
    1. Winnebago Indians — Juvenile fiction. [1. Winnebago
Indians — Fiction. 2. Indians of North America — Fiction. 3.
Grandfathers — Fiction. 4. Survival — Fiction] I. Brouwer,
Jack, ill. II. Title. III. Amazing Indian children series.
    PZ7.T3696KU   1989   [Fic]   89-15074
ISBN 0-8010-8891-7 (Baker Book House)
ISBN 0-8010-8892-5 (Baker Book House: pbk.)
ISBN 1-880114-04-6 (Grandview Publishing Company)
ISBN 1-880114-03-8 (Grandview Publishing Company: pbk.)

Printed in the United States of America

Kunu

Amazing Indian Children series:

Naya Nuki: Shoshoni Girl Who Ran
Om-kas-toe: Blackfeet Twin Captures an
    Elkdog
Soun Tetoken: Nez Perce Boy Tames a
    Stallion
Kunu: Winnebago Boy Escapes
Pathki Nana: Kootenai Girl Solves a Mystery
Moho Wat: Sheepeater Boy Attempts a
    Rescue

To the over six hundred Winnebago
men, women, and children
who died during the "Removal"
and subsequent escape from Crow Creek.

With special thanks to:
The boys and girls of Kelly Elementary School
in Kelly, Wyoming
Deputy Sheriff Dave Thorson, Jackson, Wyoming
KSGT Radio in Jackson, Wyoming
The Minnesota Historical Society
Mickey Scott
Dr. Nancy Oestreich Lurie

Contents

Preface 9

1. Danger at Dawn 13

2. Death in Sight 23

3. Running for Life 31

4. Captured! 41

5. Thirty–eight Die 53

6. Chokay's Plan 63

7. Great Misery 73

8. Thirteen Terrible Days 85

9. Working in Secret 97

10. A Treasure on the Missouri 109

11. One More Night 121

12. A Risky Escape 133

13. Overboard! 145

14. Kunu's Bravery 155

15. A Dream Comes True 167

Epilogue 181

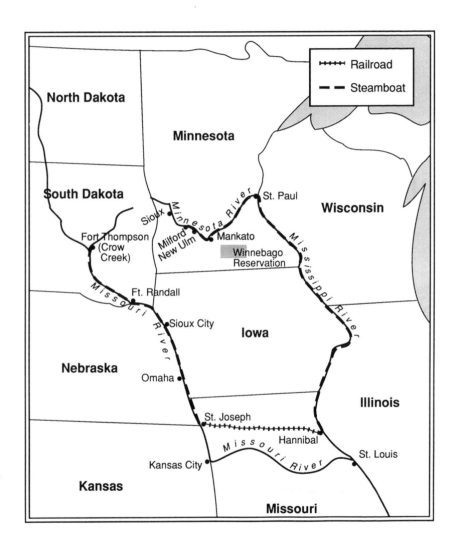

Preface

Alberta Day was the inspiration for this book. She lives in the Wisconsin Dells and is a mother and a grandmother who loves her family and her Winnebago people. Alberta is concerned that many of her people do not know much about the story of how their ancestors were forced from their land and homes in Blue Earth County, Minnesota, in 1863. "Our people must not forget their past and how their ancestors had to suffer great hardships and loss."

Alberta talked to me nonstop for ninety minutes in August 1987. After I listened to her moving words, I had no doubt that a book about the Winnebago people should be written as a small contribution to their legacy.

While describing the injustices suffered by the Winnebagoes, Alberta also told about white people who secretly helped a few of her people to escape the forced removal. Some Indians were hidden on farms. Others were even given small parcels of land and protected by the white land owners. Such rescues were the exception, however.

Kunu (ko͞o-no͞o) is a fictional character. In the Winnebago language his name means "first-born son." Like many other men of that day, Kunu's father was absent from his family. He was fighting in the Union Army in the Civil War. That is why Kunu had to assume adult responsibilities. When their survival depended on escape from Crow Creek, many Winnebago people literally walked away, heading south along the banks of the Missouri River. Those unable to walk escaped in dugout boats. Kunu's grandfather was one of them. He needed his grandson to help him with his escape in a cottonwood tree dugout.

He-cho-kay-ha is Winnebago for *grandfather* and is shortened to *Chō-kāy* for easier reading.

My challenge in writing this book was to make it as realistic as possible. Exploring the Minnesota River, the Mississippi River, the State of Missouri from Hannibal to St. Joseph, and the Missouri River from St. Louis to Crow Creek gave me a clear image of the geography involved in this story. Reading as much as I could find about the actual events increased my understanding of those awful days in 1862–63.

I hope this story will, in a small way, help to fulfill Alberta's desire for her people to better understand and appreciate their past.

1

Danger at Dawn

Kunu was really happy. He had looked forward to this short trip for a long time. The ten-year-old boy was with Chokay, the Winnebago Indian word for grandfather. His dog, Wakee, ran beside him. Most exciting of all, Kunu was riding a beautiful white horse along the bank of a quiet river and feeling quite grown up.

Kunu had no way of knowing that in just a few days his happiness would change to fear. His whole life would change. Nothing could stop the terrible things that were coming in the days ahead.

Chokay and Kunu were taking a string of six beautiful horses to Mr. J. C. Dickinson, who ran a boarding house at the headquarters of the Lower Sioux Indian Agency in Minnesota. It was August of 1862. As he rode along at the end of the line of horses, Kunu thought about his father, a volunteer soldier in Abraham Lincoln's army. A great Civil War was being fought many miles away.

Kunu missed his father. Often the boy would not eat any food for days. Fasting was the Winnebago way to let Earthmaker know their thoughts and prayers. Kunu fasted for his father, whom he loved so much. He prayed to Earthmaker to keep his father safe in battle. He prayed that his father would come home soon.

Chokay rode on Old Horse at the front of the line. Grandfather had had Old Horse since she was a filly. These days, Chokay's legs got very sore. When he walked very far, his ankles and knees swelled up badly. Then he would begin limping and walking would become very painful. But Grandfather's arms were still strong and powerful. His eyes were good and his mind full of great wisdom.

Kunu loved his grandfather very, very much. The older man taught his grandson many things about life on this earth. The boy would sit for hours listening to Chokay tell stories. Kunu especially loved the tales about hunting and about the wars against the Winnebagoes' enemies. There were also stories about good deeds. Chokay told Kunu how men and women would give away everything to help family and friends. He taught Kunu to be honest, generous, and brave. The boy remembered everything his grandfather told him.

This trip to the Lower Sioux Agency on the Minnesota River would take three days. The old man and the boy camped near the river on the first night. The second night they stayed with Chokay's friends near the town of Milford, Minnesota. This family had come to America from Germany. Chokay had once helped them move their belongings from Mankato to Milford. They had been Chokay's friends ever since.

Many German people had settled in Milford. This family had a small farm. They had an eleven-year-old son named Karl. Although Karl and Kunu had seen each other only two times before this visit, they were already good friends.

Karl helped Kunu take the horses to the pasture next to the small farmhouse. Then Kunu helped Karl feed the pigs and the chickens. Karl's mother had prepared a delicious meal for her family and their Indian friends. Kunu liked to hear Karl and his parents talk. They spoke with an accent that seemed strange to him.

After supper there was time for the two boys to play outside. There was a rope swing hanging at one end of the barn. The rope was tied to the overhanging part of the roof outside the back of the barn. Karl's dad had installed the rope to lift hay up to the second-floor opening of the loft.

The rope made a perfect swing, and the boys took turns swinging. Karl was taller than Kunu and had great strength. He could push Kunu high above his head. They pushed each other over and over again. Kunu liked to have Karl give him a twist to make him spin around and around. The boys laughed and hollered as they swung. Chokay spent the time talking to Karl's mother and father in the cozy farmhouse.

Kunu and Chokay spent the night camped in the barn. Kunu's faithful dog, Wakee, slept next to the boy in the soft hay. After a big breakfast of eggs, potatoes, and German sausage, Chokay and Kunu tied the horses in a line, said good-bye, and rode away. Kunu had no idea that his next visit to this farm would be an unbelievably sad experience.

That same afternoon, Chokay led Kunu and the horses up to the boarding house at the Lower Sioux Agency. Mr. Dickinson came out to meet them and motioned for Chokay to follow him to the corral in back of the big house. Then the man gave Chokay some money from his pocket, said a few words, and went back into the house.

"Let's go home, Kunu. Want to ride or walk?"

"I'll walk, Chokay. I can go as fast as Old Horse."

It was a beautiful Sunday afternoon. Grandfather rode straight to the Indian Agency's general store. Kunu held Old Horse's reins while Chokay went inside. The boy watched people move about slowly in the warm sun. He kept Wakee close by his side because he knew there were several big dogs around that did not like a strange dog coming into their territory. (The name *Wakee* in Winnebago means "raccoon." Kunu had chosen that name because the dog had a mask of black around each eye, making him look like a raccoon.)

There were lots of Sioux Indians coming and going around the Agency. They seemed strange to Kunu. He wondered why they spoke a different language and why they were so different from his own people.

Chokay came quickly out of the general store with the things he had bought. Grandfather handed Kunu a large piece of chocolate but said nothing. The old man simply pulled himself onto Old Horse and rode away from the store.

The two travelers did not speak. Kunu was enjoying his chocolate. Chokay sat quietly and rode toward the trees near the Minnesota River. His face was hidden from Kunu. Finally, in a small clearing near the river, Kunu's grandfather slid to the ground and motioned for the boy to come closer. Kunu saw that Chokay's face had a very troubled look.

"Kunu, our Sioux brothers are full of hate for the white man," said Chokay. "My heart tells me that bad things will happen soon. We will camp here for the night. Before the sun shines on our beds, we will be on the trail for home."

The two of them had traveled lightly. Bedrolls and a sack of food had been tied to Old Horse's saddle. Kunu and Chokay each carried a knife. Grandfather had a flint and a piece of metal to spark their fires.

"Chokay, why do the Sioux hate the white man?" asked Kunu as they prepared their simple campsite.

"Kunu, their hatred is like a giant fire that grows larger and larger. It has been burning for years. Many of our people also hate the whites. Some Indian Agents have cheated and robbed Indian people. These evil men take our cloth, our food, our seed, and even our land. They lie to us. They break our treaties. We sell them our land, and they do not pay us. Now our crops are dying in the field. Rain has not fallen from the sky for many days. Our children and old people are hungry. Still the Agents lie and cheat us."

"Chokay, do you hate the white man?" Kunu wondered aloud.

"White man or Indian, my son, either man can be good or bad. Each man shows me his heart, which can carry friendship or hate. When you become a man, you will learn to read the hearts of many people. If your own heart is good, many people will be your friends."

Once again Kunu heard great wisdom from his grandfather, yet Chokay's words were clear and simple. Although even Kunu could understand the way grown men behaved, he still wondered why hate could grow so fast and in so many hearts at once.

After a supper of dried corn, wild raspberries, and dried meat, Kunu ate the last of his delicious chocolate. As it grew dark, the boy and his dog walked down to the edge of a creek for a cool drink of water. With Wakee sitting next to him, Kunu sat looking into the moving water. He wondered about all Chokay had just told him. Karl and his parents were white people. But they were good, so no Indian should hate them. The boy had many new thoughts to take home with him from this trip.

Back at the campsite Kunu and Wakee lay down in the soft grass to sleep. Then Grandfather spoke softly, but what he told Kunu would keep the boy awake for many

hours. "Kunu, there will be great trouble in this land before we reach our home. Our Sioux brothers burn with hatred. In the morning we must leave this place early."

Great trouble before we reach our home. Those words filled Kunu's thoughts. He could not lie still. The boy rolled over and over again. He could not get comfortable. Great trouble? What kind of trouble? Would there be danger? Would there be fighting?

Kunu stroked Wakee's back. The dog licked the boy's face. After many twists and turns, sleep finally came, but Kunu dreamed many dreams. Chokay heard his grandson call out loud many times as the boy slept fitfully, disturbed by news of the trouble soon to come.

2

Death in Sight

In the middle of a dream, Kunu felt his grandfather's strong hand shake him by the shoulder. It was still dark when the boy opened his eyes. He heard Chokay saying, "Kunu, it is time to leave. Bring Old Horse. Daylight will be here soon. I wish to go from this place."

The boy felt tired and stiff. His sleep had not been peaceful. Kunu rubbed his eyes. The sky was dark and heavy with clouds. It would be hard to find Old Horse. The boy walked slowly through the trees and stopped often to listen. Old Horse would be heard before she could be seen.

Kunu could not find Old Horse. He walked in a circle around the camp. Then he would walk another circle, each one bigger than the last.

"Kunu, hurry! We must be leaving," Chokay called, and his words brought the boy back to the campsite.

"Old Horse is gone, Chokay. I found her hobble rope. It fell from her legs."

"Daylight is coming, my grandson. Go again. She cannot be far. Find my horse and return quickly."

Grandfather had the bedrolls tied tightly and ready to go. He handed Kunu some dried meat and two biscuits to take with him. They boy ate the food as he walked. It was light enough to see a little now. Kunu took Wakee along to help in the search for the missing horse.

"Find Old Horse, Wakee. Find her!" the boy said as they disappeared into the trees.

The sky was getting brighter every minute. Soon the sun would be above the eastern hills. Kunu returned to the place where he had found the hobble rope. He remembered tying the rope to Old Horse's front legs so the animal could not walk very far from the camp. The knot must have loosened, he thought.

Kunu walked farther and farther from the camp but still could not find Old Horse. As soon as he picked up the horse's trail, he would quickly lose it again. Finally the boy heard a horse cough. He started toward the sound, then came to a sudden stop when he heard another sound. It was a booming sound. Gunshots! Those were gunshots!

Kunu stopped. He stood very still. "Probably a hunter," the boy said to himself. Before he could take another step, more shots were fired. They were coming from the direction of the Indian Agency buildings. Kunu was sure of that much. Then many more shots rang out in the morning air. Although he did not know it yet, Kunu was listening to the beginning of an awful uprising, a massacre. He turned and dashed back to where Chokay was waiting.

"Chokay, there is shooting! It's coming from the Agency! What does it mean?"

"Stay with me. We will see," said his grandfather. Kunu had never seen Chokay move faster. The short stocky man took long running strides through the dense trees. He did not limp at all. The boy had to run his hardest to keep up.

Suddenly Chokay stopped and they both looked between two trees across open land. Not far from this place an Agency building was on fire. People were running in every direction as Sioux warriors calmly took aim and fired. Right in front of them, Chokay and Kunu saw two white men fall to the ground.

"Kunu, come. We, too, must run!" Chokay cried, as he turned and disappeared into the trees.

Kunu was terrified. He felt numb. He stood absolutely still as his eyes fastened on the awful sight before him.

"Kunu!" yelled Chokay from a distance. The old man stopped when he did not see the boy behind him. Finally Kunu turned his head from the scene. He would never forget what he had just seen. Two men had died while he stood so near. It was a horrible sight!

Chokay headed back to the campsite. Kunu was able to catch up easily since his grandfather moved more slowly now. He was limping badly. At the camp the old man lowered himself to his knees. His arms braced his body as he rolled over onto his back. Chokay stretched

his legs straight out on the soft leaves covering the ground.

"Kunu, we have seen great trouble," he sighed. "The fires of hate are burning out of control."

"Chokay, what will happen next? What can we do?"

"My son, we are in great danger. We should not be here. Our Sioux brothers do a bad thing. Many will die. We must get back to our people. First you must find Old Horse. I cannot walk. The running has caused my legs to hurt greatly. Go! Find our horse! Hurry! We must leave before we are found here!"

Kunu and Wakee ran to the place where they had heard Old Horse cough. Not far from that spot the boy picked up the animal's trail. This time it was easy to follow. The tracks led to the river and showed that the horse had broken into a gallop when she heard the loud gunshots.

The boy ran on and on. All he could think about was the sight of the two men running for their lives. Then had come the shots and both men had fallen silently to the ground. That scene went through the boy's mind over and over again.

How long he ran, Kunu did not know. He just moved like a machine, paying attention only to the trees, the roots, and the rocks he had to miss. Suddenly the boy's thoughts were interrupted by Wakee's barking.

"Wakee! Where are you? I forgot about you," Kunu added softly and then stopped to listen. The barking was louder. Kunu ran toward the sound. "Wakee, I'm coming," the boy said to himself. "Keep barking."

Kunu slowed to a walk when he saw his faithful dog. Right in front of the dog stood Old Horse. The big mare was breathing hard. White foam oozed from her mouth. Each time the horse tried to walk away, Wakee jumped in her path and barked loudly. The dog was holding the much larger animal in her place.

"Good dog," Kunu said softly. The boy walked slowly and carefully toward the frightened horse. "Take it easy. Take it easy," Kunu said to the nervous animal.

The boy moved slowly up to the mare. He rubbed her nose with his left hand and talked to her in a quiet voice. With his right hand, Kunu took a coil of rope from his shoulder. He looped the rope around Old Horse's neck and held her firmly. The trip back to the campsite took a long time. Old Horse had a bad cut on her left hind leg and was limping a little.

Chokay was glad to see his grandson return with the horse. "Kunu, you have done well. Quickly, we must leave. The fighting continues. We must not be seen by anyone. We will stay away from the roads. We will follow the trails made by deer. We cannot stop until we are safely away from this place."

Kunu went first. He stayed in the tall bushes and trees. The boy picked his way along as fast as he could go. He paid no attention as many branches scraped his head and scratched his face. Old Horse followed closely behind Kunu. Grandfather rode, leaning forward and sweeping his eyes from side to side. Chokay was on the lookout for danger.

Kunu hoped Old Horse could keep going. Their lives might depend on the weak animal who had served Chokay so well all these years. Kunu's legs seemed to be stronger than ever. Now the boy would show his grandfather his strength and bravery. He would give every ounce of his energy to help them both get home safely. Kunu would prove he was ready to be a man.

3

Running for Life

Following trails made by deer was slow and not easy. It was not until late that Monday afternoon, August 18, 1862, that Kunu saw the familiar farm of their German friends. He stood at the edge of the forest and looked across an open field. There was the barn and Karl's house. The rope the boys had used for a swing hung limply from the barn's eaves. No one was in sight.

"Stand very still, Grandson. Something is wrong. Stay hidden." Chokay's words made Kunu feel strangely hollow inside.

The boy's legs had been moving for hours without a rest. They felt like they did not want to stop. But Kunu waited while Chokay slid silently from Old Horse's back. He stood close to Kunu as they both peered out at the deserted farm. The old man took the boy by the arm and led him to two large trees.

"Chokay, look," whispered Kunu.

"I see it, too, my son," said the old man sadly.

There in the corral lay two dead cows. Before the boy could move to a place where he could see better, a Sioux warrior appeared in the farmyard between the barn and the house. Instantly three more Sioux came into view.

Kunu strained to see more. When he moved to the right just a few steps, he saw something that made his heart pound. His whole body felt weak and sick and he got dizzy. His eyes became blurry, but he knew that he had seen the bodies of Karl's mother and father lying near the Sioux braves.

Things happened fast as Kunu took in this awful sight. The four warriors split up. Two ran toward the house and two started around the barn.

Where is Karl? The warriors must be looking for him, thought Kunu.

He did not have long to wait for an answer. There in the doorway of the second-floor opening to the hayloft stood Karl. Kunu wanted to shout to warn his friend that the warriors were coming around the barn. In a few seconds they would see Karl standing there. What can I do? wondered Kunu. The warriors will see him. Karl will die. I must help him.

Just then Chokay grabbed Kunu by the arm. He signaled his grandson to remain silent. The two of them saw Karl spot the warriors coming and then duck back into the hayloft. The two warriors jerked the lower doors open and ran into the barn.

When the Sioux disappeared inside, Karl grabbed the rope and slid down to the ground. As soon as his feet hit the ground, Karl was running for his life. He headed straight for the cornfield and disappeared in the tall stalks. Seconds later the two warriors charged out of the barn. The rope Karl used was still swinging back and forth. One warrior looked up at the hayloft. The other

brave pointed to the ground. Karl's tracks were plainly marked in the damp dirt.

The two warriors shouted to the two who had gone toward the farmhouse. Soon all four were racing into the cornfield at top speed.

Chokay grabbed Kunu by the arm again and the two of them ran to a place where the cornfield almost touched the forest. They got there at the same time that Karl came running out of the cornstalks. The terrified boy ran right into Chokay. The old man held Karl tightly and quickly covered the boy's mouth with one hand to stifle his cry.

"You know we are your friends. We are here to help you," whispered Chokay.

Kunu's grandfather told Kunu to take Karl and run east, then hide and wait for him. Before the boys could take their first step, Chokay had hold of Wakee by the back of the dog's neck. The dog had already started barking.

"Go! Find!" Chokay shouted, as he threw a rock into the trees as far west as he could fling it. Wakee bounded off through the trees after the rock, barking as loudly as he could.

Chokay turned quickly and stepped into the opening between the forest and the field just before the Sioux braves burst out of the cornstalks. The startled warriors stopped in front of the old man, only inches away.

"I am Winnebago," Chokay said. "The boy ran there. My dog chases him." The old man pointed west toward the barking sounds. Without waiting, the warriors dashed into the trees, following the barking dog.

Chokay turned around, pulled himself to Old Horse's back, and quickly headed east through the forest. He had gone just over a mile when he heard a familiar sound coming from the bushes ahead. It was a birdcall, and Chokay knew it was a signal from Kunu. When Grandfather answered with the same call, Kunu and Karl came out of the dense thicket.

Chokay jumped down from Old Horse and walked up to the two boys. With one hand on Karl's shoulder, the old man spoke softly to the confused farmboy. "Karl, you have been very brave. An awful thing has been done. We cannot talk now, but we want you to come home with us.

We will take care of you. No one will harm you. We must go quickly. We are not safe here. The Sioux warriors will follow our tracks."

"Chokay, Karl has a sore ankle. He hurt it when he slid to the ground on the rope," Kunu said.

Chokay saw the swelling but he urged Karl to walk on it as well as he could. He hoped the ankle would loosen up. Karl did well. He limped badly at first, but the ankle did feel a little better. Kunu wondered about Wakee. Had his dog led the warriors far enough? Would he get away from them? Would Kunu ever see his faithful dog again? Wakee had given Karl a chance to escape. Kunu hoped the dog would fool the warriors and return to him safely.

On and on the three traveled over the faint deer trails. They moved as fast as possible. Several times they waded in shallow streams where they would leave no tracks for the warriors to follow. At a place deep in the trees and near a spring, Chokay suddenly pulled Old Horse to a stop.

"We stop here. Darkness comes soon. The town of New Ulm is just ahead. We will rest. Before the sun returns we will pass the town and finish our journey. Old

Horse needs rest. You boys have done well. Now we eat and sleep. Tomorrow our journey ends."

Nothing more was said. Kunu tied Old Horse to a young but strong tree surrounded by grass. He found a fallen tree and sat down wearily. Kunu watched Karl try to eat some food, but he didn't eat very much. Karl said nothing. His head was down. It was hard for Karl to even look at Kunu or his grandfather.

When Kunu finally rose to his feet, he almost toppled over. His legs were weak and felt like waving blades of grass. His head was spinning. The excitement and the many hours of walking had sapped his strength. His body felt completely drained.

"Water, Kunu! You need water," said Chokay. "Your body has worked hard. You have lost much water from your skin. Drink much water from the spring." Chokay knew a great deal about life. Water did help the boy gain back some strength. Still, Kunu's legs ached and his whole body felt weary.

That night Kunu was miserable. He was tired but could not sleep. The boy wrapped his blanket around himself and sat leaning against a large tree. Wakee had not found them yet, and Kunu was worried about him. The boy listened to every sound of the night. He could not get comfortable. He was sore all over. A cold drizzle of rain started to fall. Kunu moved to the drier side of the tree and noticed that Karl was not sleeping either. It was a long, long night for the two boys.

Kunu's mind raced with many thoughts and questions. Much had happened since he heard those first gunshots at the Indian Agency. How he wished his father could be here with him. What could his father be doing? When would he come home from the army? What was going to happen to Karl? Would they make it home the next day? Would his mother and sisters be safe? Would this new trouble spread to his people and to his home?

With thoughts like those, how could anyone sleep! But the Winnebago boy did doze off several times in the early morning hours. Chokay's voice sounded like part of his grandson's dreams: "Kunu, Karl, wake up. We go now."

Grandfather seemed ready to leave. Kunu fetched Old Horse, while Chokay and Karl made up the bedrolls. Old Horse was still tied securely to the sturdy tree. Rain continued off and on. It was cold and damp in the morning darkness, but the more Kunu kept moving, the better he felt.

Karl was limping badly. His ankle was swollen to twice its normal size. The boy still said nothing. All three had eaten their dried corn and dried meat in silence.

"We must be careful today," warned Chokay. "There may be trouble at New Ulm. While it is still dark, we will pass by the town in the trees to the south." His grandfather's words made it sound easy, so Kunu was ready to do his part again today.

The wise old man was right. The trouble was spreading. Sioux warriors were already moving toward the town of New Ulm. All along the Minnesota River, the Sioux were attacking farmers, travelers, and any other white people they could find. Many would die. On this Tuesday, August 19, 1862, the citizens of New Ulm would have to fight for their lives.

4

Captured!

This morning, the route over the deer trails seemed easier for Kunu. Karl's limp was not as bad. Although his ankle was still swollen, Karl never complained. Kunu looked forward to getting home that day, but his dog was still missing. The boy was afraid he would never see Wakee again. The dog had saved Karl's life. Kunu was proud of him and hoped Wakee would still make it home somehow.

The three travelers passed New Ulm as the eastern sky was getting light. They hurried by as fast as possible, although they did not know that it would be the middle of the afternoon before the Sioux attacked the town.

No one spoke. Each one concentrated on the trail ahead, searching for the best way through the trees and bushes. They were very careful when they crossed the Cottonwood River because there were lots of gullies and streambeds to go through. Old Horse followed slowly, and Chokay had to urge the animal to keep going. As they were climbing out of a deep ravine, the boys had to hold on to small trees to pull themselves up the steep bank.

Kunu was the first to reach the top of the steep bank. He stood for a few seconds to catch his breath. Suddenly he had a strange feeling. Something was wrong. Something was about to happen! He was sure someone was watching him.

The first thing Kunu saw to prove he was right was the large bush in front of him. It seemed to move. The boy's eyes fastened on its leaves and branches. Then he saw a hand. It was moving. Instantly the branches parted and a warrior jumped out. Then another and another came bursting out of the nearby bushes and trees.

Kunu was quickly surrounded by Sioux warriors. Their faces, arms, and chests were painted with bright warpaint. One man grabbed Kunu by the arm. Another snatched Old Horse's reins from Chokay's hands. None of them said a word.

Kunu didn't know what to do. Everything happened too fast. He felt like running. His hands got sweaty and his throat was dry. What will happen now? he wondered. What will they do to us? Wait! Where is Karl? His friend was not in sight. What happened to Karl? He must be hiding in the ravine, Kunu guessed.

Kunu looked at Chokay. The old man's face was calm and showed no fear. Grandfather was looking at the excited warriors as if nothing unusual were happening. Without a word, Chokay jumped down and walked straight to the warrior holding Old Horse's reins. He took the reins from the Sioux and tied the horse to a small tree.

Chokay turned and faced the Sioux men. He spoke to them in their own language. One by one, he looked each warrior in the eye as he spoke. Then the old man turned toward the ravine and called, "My son, come up. Stand by me. Your legs are tired."

Kunu could not believe it. Chokay was letting the Sioux know about Karl. Why didn't his grandfather leave him hidden? They will kill Karl when they see he is white. Why are you doing this, Chokay? But Kunu kept his thoughts to himself.

The first warrior who saw Karl began shouting loudly. He waved his arms and ran toward the frightened boy. Kunu watched as Chokay instantly moved between the warrior and the startled white boy. Chokay stood facing the warrior for what seemed a long time. Finally the old man stepped forward, forcing the Sioux man to move back.

Then Chokay began speaking, but Kunu did not understand the Sioux words that flowed from his grandfather's lips. Chokay spoke in a steady, firm voice. The longer the old man spoke, the quieter the warriors became. The words seemed to roll off Chokay's lips like a poem or the words to a song. It was as if these words had been inside the old Indian for a long time, just waiting to come out.

Chokay talked and talked. When he finished, the warriors stepped back. They talked quietly among themselves. Kunu realized they were deciding about Karl and also what to do with Chokay and Kunu.

So many questions ran through Kunu's mind. Will they let us go? Will they kill Karl? Do they know who he is? Will they take us with them? Will they kill all of us? What did Chokay say to them? What should we do next? Kunu knew he would find out the answers soon.

The Sioux men finally stopped talking. They turned to face Chokay. When their leader spoke, Kunu wished he could understand what the man was saying. He could see that the two youngest warriors were not very happy. The boy could read the hate and disgust in their eyes.

When the Sioux leader finished, Chokay said a few more words to them. Again his voice was strong and calm. He looked each warrior straight in the eye. After his last words in the Sioux language, Chokay turned and untied Old Horse and said, "My sons, we go now to our home. Our Sioux brothers go their way."

No more was said by anyone. In seconds the warriors were gone from sight. The boys followed Old Horse as

Chokay rode her away. They looked back many times to see if they were being followed. Kunu was anxious to get away from that place as fast as possible. He hoped he soon would hear Chokay tell the words he used to get the warriors to let them go on their way.

Grandfather did not stop or speak for hours. At last a rest stop was made by a stream. Chokay let Old Horse take a long drink. He told Kunu and Karl to rest, eat, and drink lots of fresh water.

"Chokay, what words did you speak to the warriors?" Kunu asked. "Why did you let Karl come from his hiding place? Are we safe now?" Kunu wanted to ask many more questions, but grandfather started to speak.

"You have many questions, my son. I will tell the whole story when we get home. I told the Sioux warriors that Karl is my adopted son and that he lives with me as a part of my family. I told the Sioux that we must get home to tell our people of the trouble and to tell our chiefs that our Sioux brothers need the help of all the Winnebago people in their war against the white men. I told them to do nothing that would make our people their enemies. To harm Karl, my adopted son, would cause them much trouble with all the Winnebago people."

"Chokay, will our people help the Sioux fight the white men? Can the white men be defeated? Will Karl live with us? For how long?" Kunu's questions poured from him.

His grandfather silenced Kunu with a wave of his hand. "We talk no more. Before another sun rises we must be home. Answers to all questions will come then."

The three travelers continued on in silence. Except for several thunderstorms, nothing delayed their progress. Just before darkness settled over the land, Chokay changed directions and headed toward a road he knew. This route led to the Winnebago Reservation in Blue Earth County.

The rest of the journey was easy. Soon Kunu saw many familiar sights. Oil lamps burned in the homes along the road. His own home was dark when the three finally reached the front door. Kunu led Karl into the small house. His father had built it very recently. Before the floor was done, Kunu's father had left for the Union Army and the white man's war. The dirt floor was covered here and there with reed mats.

Kunu's mother greeted the tired travelers and welcomed Karl warmly. While Chokay quickly explained what had happened, Kunu's mother fixed some delicious soup. She heated some dry corn cakes to go with the soup. Everyone spoke softly so as not to wake the two younger children. Kunu's two little sisters slept together in a small room in the back of the house. That night Kunu and Karl slept soundly.

Word about the Sioux attacks had spread quickly throughout the land. The story of Chokay, Kunu, and Karl was also passed on from person to person. The most exciting day for Kunu came three days after their return home. Kunu and Karl were walking back from the field where they had been picking corn all morning. Karl was the first to notice an animal lying in the grass near the road. As the two boys approached the animal, Kunu started to run. He couldn't believe his eyes. It was Wakee! The dog pulled himself to his feet and limped toward Kunu, wagging his tail slowly.

Kunu dropped to his knees and hugged the exhausted dog. He quickly examined the leg that Wakee limped on so badly. The boy found a huge thorn embedded deep inside the dog's paw. Kunu gripped the thorn in his teeth and pulled it out cleanly. Wakee let out a soft cry.

Kunu picked up the dog, carried him into the house, and gave him food and water. Wakee would sleep for most of the next three days. The dog was completely worn out from his journey home.

A few of the Winnebago chiefs thought that their people should help the Sioux fight the white men, but most said it would be bad. The older men especially argued against any fighting. They said that only bad things would come to their people in a war against the white men. In the end, the Winnebago people did not fight. The chiefs told their people to stay far from the fighting. Most listened, although some of the young men did not stay away.

The Sioux warriors fought hard for over a month. On September 23, 1862, at Wood Lake near the Upper Sioux Agency, Colonel Henry Sibley and his troops defeated the Sioux in a fierce battle. This ended the organized fighting. Hundreds of Indians surrendered. The brief war was ending.

Over five hundred white civilians and soldiers had been killed in the uprising. No one knows how many Sioux died. Hundreds of Indians were captured or surrendered. For the next thirty years there would be other wars between the Native Americans and the invading white men.

For Kunu and all the Winnebago people, the war that had just ended would change their lives forever. That September, no one could even imagine the terrible things that would happen in the spring and summer of 1863.

5

Thirty-eight Die

Kunu and Karl had stayed close to home during the uprising. When it was all over, 303 Sioux warriors were sentenced to be hanged. Some of their trials lasted only five minutes. Many white people wanted them hanged immediately. Everyone seemed either angry or scared. Everything had changed. Now only Chokay went to the city of Mankato. Each time he returned, he had the latest news.

When President Lincoln heard that so many Sioux men would be hanged, he ordered a delay. The president had two men work full-time to study all the cases. While this was happening, 1,700 Sioux men, women, and children were marched to Fort Snelling near present-day St. Paul, Minnesota. On the way there, many white people tried to attack the Indians with guns, knives, clubs, and rocks. Soldiers often had to form a human wall to hold back the angry whites.

Kunu heard the awful stories of the fighting, the prison camps, and the hatred that filled the hearts of many people. He never talked to Karl about these things. Karl was still very quiet. He hardly said a word to anyone except Kunu. Chokay had told Karl that he could stay with Kunu as long as he wanted to. Kunu's grandfather also said he would try to find the aunt and uncle Karl had mentioned. But it might be very difficult, since no Indian was welcome anywhere near Milford or any other place where warfare had taken place.

It was early in December of 1862 that Chokay made a most important visit to Mankato. On this trip Chokay heard about the message that had just come from President Lincoln. Not all the 303 imprisoned Sioux men would be hanged. Only thirty-nine would meet that fate. They would all die at the same instant on the day after Christmas.

Something happened on this visit that brought Chokay much happiness. When the old man went to the Mankato general store to buy supplies, the storekeeper told Chokay that a man with a German accent had come in the store asking about him. The stranger had told the storekeeper that he was staying in the hotel just one block from the store.

When Chokay heard that the man sounded German, he went straight to the hotel to find him. The hotel clerk sent the bellhop to get the German man from his room. As soon as Chokay saw the man come into the hotel lobby, he knew who he was. It must be Karl's uncle! The man looked much like Karl's father, but was a little taller and thinner.

"Thank you for coming to see me," the man said to Chokay. "People at the store say you knew my nephew, Karl, and his parents. They say you have a German boy living with you now. Is this boy my nephew? I have been looking for Karl for over two months. I have prayed that he was alive and well, but I was losing hope."

Chokay smiled and said, "Karl is fine. He is living with us. We took him with us when he escaped the Sioux warriors. I just left him yesterday to come to Mankato."

"Thank God! Thank God! And thank you, my friend," added Karl's uncle. "You have done a great thing. Thank you. Thank you so much."

The man's eyes were watery. His voice became shaky with emotion. When he calmed down, Karl's uncle asked Chokay all about the boy's escape and the journey to Chokay's people. Next he asked where Chokay lived and how soon he could go there to see his nephew.

Chokay said, "We will leave for my home as soon as you are ready. Karl's heart will fill with joy when he sees you. The boy has been full of sorrow and fear every day. He needs you very much."

"I have a wagon and a fine team. You can tie your horse to the back of my wagon and ride next to me," Karl's uncle told Chokay.

It took Karl's uncle only a short time to harness his two horses to the wagon. Chokay tied Old Horse to the back, loaded his supplies, and climbed aboard. The two men talked every minute of their trip.

It was early evening when the team of horses pulled the wagon up to Kunu's house. Kunu and Karl had been walking up to the back door when they saw the wagon turn off the road.

"Look, Chokay comes home in a wagon. Who is with him?" Kunu asked.

Karl seemed hardly interested until he heard something that set his heart pounding with excitement. He heard his name being called as only a German-speaking person would say it. Then he heard the man driving the wagon speak in perfect German. Karl broke into a dead run. Kunu had not seen Karl run that fast since the Sioux warriors had chased him through the cornstalks. Karl got to the wagon before Kunu had made it halfway there.

Karl's uncle leaped to the ground. He picked up Karl and spun him around and around, holding him as tight as he could. German words poured from the man. Karl couldn't even speak. For the first time since his parents were killed, Karl cried and cried. He coughed and sobbed for a long time. Kunu stood back. He knew this reunion was a great moment for his friend.

Kunu was both happy and sad. He knew what was going to happen before anyone had told him. Karl would leave

with his uncle. He would not be living with Kunu any more. They might never see each other again!

When Karl and his uncle left on the very next day, many Winnebago people came to say farewell. Some gave Karl small gifts. Kunu gave his friend his prized possession, a beautiful otter fur. "Karl, take this fur," he said. "It will remind you of the time we were brothers together. I will always be your brother."

The white boy could not speak, but he managed a smile and shook Kunu's hand. Karl turned and climbed onto the wagon. Before Karl's uncle climbed up to his seat, he walked over to Chokay. He reached out to shake the older man's wrinkled hand. He did not let it loose the whole time he spoke. "You have saved Karl's life. You have done a wonderful thing. Someday I hope we can help you. We will never forget what you have done. If a day ever comes when you need us, we will be ready to help you. Thank you, my friend."

Then Karl's uncle turned and climbed to his seat on the wagon. He took the reins and signaled the horses to go. Karl looked back at Kunu. For the first time since his parents had been killed, the boy had a real smile on his face.

Karl waved to Kunu as the wagon went around a turn in the road and out of sight.

"Kunu, many things have changed. The killing has made dark valleys between Indians and whites. Only Earthmaker knows what will happen in the days ahead. My grandson will learn his place in Earthmaker's plan. Be strong. Be honest. Fast often and pray. You can do great things with your life."

Chokay's words filled Kunu's mind. He would not forget them. His grandfather's words would follow the boy and prepare him for the important events that would start happening very soon.

December 26 was only a short time away. That was the day when thirty-nine brave men were scheduled to die. The hangings would happen in the Mankato town square. In the prison, missionaries had prayed with the doomed Indian men. Many were baptized.

One of the condemned warriors took time to write a letter to his father-in-law, who was a Sioux chief. The letter tells how he and the other young men felt as they waited to die:

You deceived me, my chief. You said if we followed the advice of General Sibley, and gave ourselves up to the whites, all would be well. You said no innocent man would be hurt. I have not killed or wounded a whiteman or any white person. I did not steal their property. Yet today I am set apart to be hanged and must die in a few days, while men who are guilty will remain in prison.

My wife is your daughter. My children are your grandchildren. I leave them in your care and under your protection. Do not let them suffer. When my children are grown up, let them know that their father died because he followed the advice of his chief, and without having the blood of a whiteman to answer for to the Great Spirit.

My wife and children are dear to me. Let them not grieve for me. Let them remember that the brave should be prepared to meet death, and I will do as becomes a Sioux.[1]

In Mankato, that day after Christmas, the sentenced Sioux men died by hanging. At the last minute one man was pardoned. But thirty-eight Indians died.

Kunu heard his people talk about the hangings. They talked about their fear of the white people. The Winnebago

1. From *The Sioux Uprising of 1862* by Kenneth Carley (© Minnesota Historical Society 1961/1976), pages 72–73.

people did not yet know about the secret society that was being formed. Called "The Knights of the Forest," this society of white men was working to get all Indian people out of Minnesota forever. This did not mean just the Sioux, but Winnebago Indians also. This society did not care whether the Winnebago people were innocent. They just wanted Minnesota for white people only.

Angry people were everywhere. The hatred toward all Indians was talked about openly in every city and town. Only the missionaries and a few other white people dared say that the Indians should be treated fairly. Even the newspapers printed lies and hate about the Winnebago people.

It all happened so fast! The Winnebago people could not believe the news they heard. It was spring. Their fields were all plowed and some were planted. On April 25, 1863, the United States Indian Agent, Mr. Balcombe, called a council of all Winnebago chiefs. He told them that the president had signed an order to move all of them from their homes to somewhere on the Missouri River, outside of Minnesota.

6

Chokay's Plan

Move from our homes! Leave Minnesota! Move to somewhere on the Missouri River! Where? Why? Kunu could not understand. He wanted answers to his questions.

The Winnebago people would find only one answer: move willingly or at the end of a rifle. No one talked about anything else. Young men wanted to fight. Old men knew it was no use. They knew that many of their strongest braves were away fighting in President Lincoln's army. The old men warned that the white men were everywhere—like the stars in the sky. "We cannot win," they said. "Only death and suffering would come to our people if we fight. We must do what the white man tells us to do."

Kunu waited to hear what his grandfather would say. Chokay would have some reassurance for him, he knew. He listened carefully to his grandfather's words.

"My grandson, you must be brave and wise. Your father is away and you must fill his moccasins. Your mother and small sisters need you. For them, moving will be very hard. I will be with you to make sure all is well, but someday, somehow, I will return to this sacred land of my ancestors. I wish to be buried with your grandmother, who is already at rest here in this sacred ground. No man can keep me from returning to the sacred lands of my Winnebago people. In my lifetime I have seen our lands taken from us many times. The white Agents have lied to us over and over again. Now they do not even ask that we talk together. They just force us to leave our homes and our newly plowed fields, even desert the sacred graves of those we love. All Winnebago people must be brave, my son. Earthmaker will be with us."

Kunu wondered at Chokay's words. How and when would his grandfather get back to this land? If he did come back, where would he live? But the boy knew his grandfather meant what he said. He knew Chokay would do exactly what he said he would do.

A few Winnebago people had heard about the Missouri River country. They said it was a bad area. There was not much wood. It was cold. Farmland was poor. Kunu heard that he had only ten days left in the home that his father had built so recently. Ten days! And then all the Winnebago people would have to report to a camp in Mankato. From there they would start their journey away from their homes and out of Minnesota.

Three days before Kunu had to leave, he heard something that filled him with more anger and even bitter hatred. It happened while the boy was helping his mother pack. Everything they would be able to take with them they would have to carry. What could not be carried would have to be left behind. Kunu was carrying a bundle to a place inside their front door where it would be ready to load on the wagon. He heard his grandfather call him to come outside.

Kunu saw that Chokay had a very serious look on his face. "Kunu, my grandson, I have heard a bad thing about our journey to the great river. Agent Balcombe has told our people that no dogs can be taken with us."

The boy could not believe what he heard. No dogs! Leave Wakee behind! No! No! They cannot make me, Kunu said to himself. They are taking our horses and our cows. They cannot have my dog!

Kunu did not speak those words aloud, but he ran to the tree where Wakee lay sleeping in the shade. The boy stroked the dog's back. The boy knelt beside his dog, staring at the animal he loved so much. Chokay moved closer. The old man stood over his grandson and understood what he was feeling. Neither said a word for several minutes. Chokay finally spoke, and what he said made Kunu feel a little better.

"Kunu, our friends are going to try to take their dogs. They will try to hide them from the soldiers. We will also try. We will take Wakee, but first we must think of a way to hide him. Think hard, Kunu. Tomorrow we will make our plans."

From that minute on, Kunu did not eat any food. He began to fast. He would not eat until there was a plan to save Wakee. His fasting time would be full of prayers to Earthmaker, to the Great Spirit that white people called God. Between his prayers, Kunu tried to think of a way to save his faithful dog. That night—Tuesday, May 5—the boy did not sleep. Kunu sat near his dog, thinking and praying.

Kunu felt miserable in the morning. He had had no sleep and no food. And still he had no plan. All he could think of was running away with Wakee. He knew he couldn't do that, however. His family needed him. He could not leave his mother, his two small sisters, and his grandfather. It was his duty to stay with them. He would take his father's place during this difficult time for his family.

Chokay asked Kunu to go outside with him that morning. Then his grandfather led the boy across the plowed fields. He did not speak until they reached the east end of their land. They stopped on the bank of the stream that flowed past their farm.

Then Chokay finally spoke. "Kunu, I have a plan for Wakee. The Sioux people were taken away on steamboats. We will be put on boats also. Many people will be on each boat and all will be carrying loads. The soldiers cannot possibly see what is in every bundle. When we go on the boat, Wakee will be on my shoulders, covered by a large blanket. I will hold his legs on each side of my neck. He will not be seen. On the boat we will stay in the middle of a crowd of people. We will keep Wakee from the eyes of the soldiers. He will never be seen."

As his grandfather spoke, Kunu's face brightened. His eyes were on Chokay every second. The boy began to feel good all over. Once again Grandfather had an answer. It would work! Kunu knew it would. If it was Chokay's plan, it would work!

That day Chokay carried Wakee on his shoulders many times. He was getting the dog ready for the real thing. He even covered Wakee with a large brown blanket for practice.

"Wakee is a good dog, Kunu. He must know that we prepare to fool the soldiers."

"Chokay, what will happen if they find Wakee?"

"I have a plan for that also, my grandson. We will see if that plan is needed in a few days."

On Friday, May 8, 1863, Kunu sat with his family in their wagon, being pulled by Old Horse. He watched as each familiar sight disappeared from view. Even then, white people were getting ready to take the Winnebago farmland, their houses, and everything the people could not carry with them.

Kunu wondered about so many things. Will I ever see my home again? Will my father know what happened and where to find us? Will Chokay really come back here someday? When will we be on our new land by the great river? What will happen to us?

While Kunu was deep in thought, no one spoke. The boy felt Wakee roll over. The dog was lying at Kunu's feet, his head resting on Kunu's ankle. More questions filled his mind. Will the soldiers see Wakee? Will they throw him from the boat? Will they kill my dog?

Kunu looked at Chokay. The old man's hands held the reins and kept Old Horse moving down the road to Mankato. Grandfather was small. His hands were wrinkled and rough. His shoulders were rounded. Kunu had seen his grandfather work all day in the fields so that by night he could hardly walk. Somehow Kunu knew that Chokay's legs burned with pain in his joints. His ankles and knees were aflame with arthritis, although neither knew the condition by that name.

The boy loved Chokay very much. He would do anything his grandfather asked him to do, and he believed that somehow Chokay would make everything work out right. Fortunately, Kunu did not realize what awful things were about to happen to his people. He never could have imagined that the months ahead would bring him close to death many times. There would be days when the boy would have to do things no Winnebago Indian boy had ever done before this time.

7

Great Misery

Kunu never did learn what happened to Old Horse and the wagon in Mankato, where Kunu and his family were herded into a crowded camp near the Minnesota River. There were Winnebago people everywhere. All of them carried heavy bundles. There were only a few canvas shelters in the camp. Most people would have to sleep on the ground in the open.

Chokay carried Wakee into Camp Porter on his shoulders. Under the blanket the dog looked like just another bundle of belongings. In the center of all the noise and confusion, Chokay sat down and lowered Wakee to the ground. Kunu, his mother, and his two sisters crowded close to Grandfather to keep the dog hidden from view. Kunu would not move from this place except to go to the bathroom. His mother and Chokay would leave one at a time to get food and water and to take the little girls for a walk.

A terrible thing happened at Camp Porter. Some young Winnebago braves were angry with the Sioux warriors because they had started the war that caused these bad things to happen to the Winnebago people. The young men took revenge by killing two Sioux men. They put their scalps on poles and carried them high so all the whites could see them. The Winnebago braves thought all the white people would be happy that the Winnebago had killed the Sioux men.

Again Chokay was the wise one. He knew what the white people would say. They would say that the Winnebago men were murderers, just like the Sioux. They would say that all Indians were bad and wild. These killings would be taken as proof that they should be driven from Minnesota.

Grandfather was right. The wild scalp dances gave the white people plenty of angry things to say: "Look! The Winnebago kill, too. No one is safe with these savages living here!" Others went further. "Get them out of our state. Tell them they will die if they ever come back. All Indians are bad. Nobody is safe with these killers around!"

Kunu heard such terrible things said about his people. He knew they were not true. Only a few warriors killed. Only a few did the scalp dance. Most of the Winnebago people were peaceful. Many had been baptized into the white man's churches. As Chokay had said, "Men are bad and good. Some are very foolish." Kunu thought that some don't think about their deeds before they do them. But he soon knew for sure that the killings made things worse, not better.

Not far from the noisy camp of 1,200 Winnebago people, three steamboats were docked on the bank of the Minnesota River. Chokay had walked over near the steamboats several times. Each time he looked at every detail of the boats. He wanted to find the best way to get on board without letting the soldiers see Wakee on his shoulders. He also wanted to find the best place to hide the dog while they were on the boat.

When loading time finally came, there was noise and confusion everywhere. Kunu was worried. In fact, he was scared, so he prayed to Earthmaker for help. The boy heard soldiers shouting orders. Soon a large crowd of Winnebago people started moving toward the boat docks. Women, children, old people, babies, some young men—all moved slowly away from the camp.

"Be ready," Chokay said to Kunu and his family. "Follow me. Stay very close. They cannot see Wakee walking with us in this crowd."

Kunu helped his mother get her bundle onto her back. His little sisters carried their small bundles and the boy lifted his own heavy load to his shoulder. About five hundred people moved at the same time. One steamboat had already been loaded. Chokay made sure that his family would be in the middle of this second large group. The loading took such a long time that the white soldiers got tired of the whole thing.

When Chokay got close to the steamboat, he dropped

to his knees. He rubbed Wakee's ears. "Good dog. Quiet, Wakee," Chokay whispered. "Quiet."

Wakee obeyed. He stood very still. Chokay bent down and put his head under the dog's stomach. Gently holding two of Wakee's legs on each side of his neck, Grandfather lifted the dog from the ground. Kunu put the blanket over Wakee and covered him completely.

Chokay calmly walked right up to the gangplank with his "bundle." The soldier standing there paid no attention at all. Kunu was relieved. "Wakee is going to make it!" he said to himself happily.

Grandfather walked up the planks to the first deck of the huge boat and then headed up a stairway to the top deck. Kunu was right behind, and no one bothered them at all. More and more people crowded the top deck. Families stayed together as much as possible. A few babies cried, but most of the people were strangely silent. Everyone realized that this was an awful moment in their lives. They were being forced from their land. Their homes were being taken from them. Their cows and horses were taken, too. All this was happening to inno-

cent people. It was a terrible time for the Winnebago Indians.

The steamboat was named the *Eolian*. Its two steam engines were powered by boilers that were fueled by burning wood. Smoke poured from the smokestacks that stood high above the top deck.

Suddenly Kunu saw the land on both shores of the river seem to move. Then he realized that the boat was on its way. The *Eolian* was starting its journey down the Minnesota River. It was headed for Fort Snelling, which was near present-day St. Paul, Minnesota. The fort was near the place where the Minnesota River flows into the Mississippi. It would take three days and two nights to get to the fort. The journey was delayed when, between the towns of Henderson and Belle Plaine, Kunu and many others on the boat were suddenly toppled over as the *Eolian* struck a sharp snag. A thirty-foot hole was torn in the hull. It took many hours to make emergency repairs.

The weather was cold and rainy. People shivered, even as they huddled close together. Everyone was hungry. Finally, stale crackers and dirty water were passed out to the starving Indians. Mothers held their babies close to keep them warm. There were scenes of misery everywhere Kunu looked. The boy wondered if things would be better at Fort Snelling, where they would be changing boats.

But it was no better at the stopover. Fort Snelling was more crowded than Camp Porter. Some Sioux warriors were there, and they wanted to fight when they saw the Winnebago braves, who were still carrying the scalps of their brothers. Soldiers had to keep the two groups apart.

A Major Hatch was in charge of the Indians at Fort Snelling. He got the next steamboats ready as fast as possible, obviously eager to get rid of this "problem" immediately. Chokay had carried Wakee off the *Eolian* without a hitch. While they waited for the next boat, Kunu stayed close to his dog and kept him well hidden in this crowded place.

The next steamboat was the *Canada*. More than seven hundred Winnebago people were jammed onto this one. There was hardly enough room to sit down. Hiding Wakee was easy, especially since there were only a few soldiers on each deck. They could not watch everything. Even when the soldiers were on guard duty, they paid little attention to the hundreds of Indian people jammed together on the wooden decks.

The *Canada* chugged out of the Minnesota River into the giant Mississippi. Kunu had never seen so much water. So wide was the river that no warrior could come close to shooting an arrow from one side to the other. There were many other boats on this great river.

The trip down the Mississippi took the Winnebago people along the borders of Minnesota, Wisconsin, Iowa, and parts of Illinois and Missouri. The boat steamed south at a steady speed. Hard crackers, stale meat, and water were given to the miserable passengers. The weather stayed cold and damp. Sleep on the hard wood was difficult. On and on they traveled, stopping only for wood to burn in the furnaces that heated water into steam.

Kunu watched his little sisters huddle together next to Mother. They never cried, but just sat silently in their misery. (Kunu's name means "first-born son." Henu is "first-born daughter," and Wehuh is "second-born daughter." His sisters were named Henu and Wehuh, to mark the order of their birth.) The boy wondered how much more suffering his small sisters would have to endure.

Chokay stood up often so his legs would not stiffen. Several of the old people got sick. Some became so weak they were not able to stand by themselves. Mothers with tiny babies were given extra crackers and water by their friends and family, but everywhere Kunu looked, he saw people suffering. He wondered when it would all end.

Five days after leaving Minnesota, the *Canada* docked at Hannibal, Missouri. The people were grateful to be able to step on solid ground again, although some of the older people and those who had been sick needed help in walking. Everyone was happy to leave the steamboat behind. They were sure nothing could be worse than the ride they had just finished.

They were wrong! The next leg of their trip would bring even greater suffering, and death to some. The seven hundred Winnebago people from the *Canada* were cold, tired, and hungry. Still they were forced to walk to the Hannibal train depot. There they were loaded into the cattle cars that were waiting on the tracks. Sixty people were forced into each car. The trip across Missouri by train was over two hundred miles. The cattle cars were noisy, smoky, dusty, and crowded. Fortunately, the train ride would be shorter than the steamboat trip. At each stop along the way, the doors to the cars were opened and Kunu saw several bodies taken out of each car. No time was allowed for the families to have a burial ceremony for loved ones who died on the journey. Their cries of grief and sorrow filled the cars as the train pulled away, leaving their dead behind.

The steamboat trip was miserable. The train ride was an even worse nightmare. But in St. Joseph, Missouri, still greater misery awaited the Winnebago people.

8

Thirteen Terrible Days

In St. Joseph, Missouri, the uprooted Indian people were kept in a large area next to another river. This river was the Missouri.

"Chokay, is this the place where we will make our new home?" Kunu asked. "This is the Missouri River, where you said we would be going."

"Kunu, our chiefs say this is not the place. We will travel north from here toward the cold winds far up the river." As he spoke, Chokay pointed to the steamboat tied to a dock in the distance. No one seemed to know how far and how long the next ride would be, but Kunu noticed the water rolling by the riverbank. The boy knew this much: the boat would be going upstream, against the current—and no boat could go very fast against that powerful water.

Kunu was right. The next leg of their trip would be like slow torture. Thirteen days on the steamboat *Westwind* would find the people crowded, cold, and hungry, day after day. More people would die during this awful ride. Saddest of all was an Indian mother giving birth to a baby girl. The woman became very ill and died just after the baby was born, probably because there was no doctor to save her. All the while, a woman with her own tiny baby sat close by. This woman took the new baby in her arms. She kept it warm and cozy. She fed the tiny girl. Other women would help her take care of this helpless orphan in the days to come.

Day after miserable day went by as the steamboat slowly worked its way up the Missouri River. Most days were cold and windy. The food was always the same: dry crackers and water, with a little dried meat now and then. Kunu shared his meager food with Wakee.

The dog slept most of the time, well hidden from the soldiers.

Every time the *Westwind* stopped to take on more wood for the furnaces, no Winnebago people were allowed to get off the boat. The farther the boat traveled, the drier the land looked. On some parts of the river Kunu saw steep banks. In other places the shoreline was low and muddy. Many creeks and smaller rivers flowed into the Missouri here and there along the way. The river was never the same. Chokay often stood at the rail and seemed to be studying the river closely. Kunu wondered what his grandfather was thinking. Why was he so interested in the river?

The pilot was pretty good at steering the large vessel around sandbars, rocks, and whole trees lying in the water. But at least once a day the boat hit something. A few times the clumsy vessel ran upon a sandbar. Then the captain would order the engines into reverse to back off the sand.

Thirteen days and suddenly it all ended! The captain turned the *Westwind* to the right-hand bank and pulled up to a crude dock. Here on the east side of the Missouri River, the Winnebago people were told to gather their things and go ashore with them.

Something very important and very dangerous happened just before Kunu and his grandfather got to the gangplanks leading to the dock. Chokay took a big chance and did something that could cause him great trouble. For days Chokay had been watching each soldier. Every one of them always stood in the same place. None of them was watching very closely. Now, just before Chokay left the boat, he would do something he had been planning to do for days.

Fastened to the wall of the cabin was an old axe. The handle was cracked. It was probably just hanging there until someone took time to put a new handle on it. Although Chokay had Wakee on his shoulders, he walked right next to the cabin wall. When he was close enough, Grandfather slipped the axe from its holder. Then Chokay quickly knelt down and snapped the handle off with his powerful hands. He slipped the axe head into his shirt and stood up again. Now Chokay held the axe under his shirt between his arm and body.

Kunu saw it all. Even with Wakee on his shoulders, Chokay was able to do this in less than thirty seconds. And Grandfather was walking right past eleven soldiers! They did not suspect a thing. Chokay passed right under the soldiers' noses with his two treasures—Wakee and a valuable axe head.

The homeless Winnebago people stepped ashore at a place called Crow Creek, which then was outside the United States. Crow Creek is in the state we now call South Dakota, but in 1863 it was still twenty-six years before South Dakota would become a state.

The Sioux people were already on shore. The army did their best to keep the two groups apart. The army pitched their tents and built a crude fence. They made the Sioux Indians stay on one side of their camp and the Winnebago on the other. At the same time, the soldiers began building a permanent fort between the two groups.

The man in charge of the Crow Creek post was Clark W. Thompson. Soon the fort would be called Fort Thompson. Kunu and his family stood with hundreds of their people and listened to Mr. Thompson speak.

"This will be your new home. There is wood to build a shelter for your family. There is land for planting potatoes, corn, and other vegetables. My men and I are here to help you. This will be your home forever. It will never be taken away from you. All of you must stay here on your own land. Anyone who tries to leave will be shot on sight. You will have good lives here. Our Great White Chief in Washington will take good care of his native children."

Our home forever . . . anyone who leaves will be shot . . . our Great White Chief will take care of us. These words and ideas were more than Kunu could understand. The boy was weary. His stomach was empty. As his eyes saw suffering people all around him, Kunu thought that Mr. Thompson spoke with hollow words.

"Kunu, everyone, come quickly!" Chokay's words startled Kunu. Grandfather was limping badly as he led his family away, although most of the people were waiting in lines for food. Chokay had heard the soldiers talking about the places the Winnebago people would be allowed to build their shelters. The wise old man wanted to have a shelter started before anything else.

"We eat later," Chokay told his family. "Now we build. The rains are cold. The winds are strong. To live we must have shelter."

Crow Creek flowed into the Missouri River from the east. The banks of the creek were lined with tall cottonwood trees. Many were alive. Some were dead. Many dead trees still stood stark against the prairie sky. Others lay on the ground and in the creek. Chokay had a plan for a quick shelter that could be made before darkness came. It would protect his family until a better house could be made.

"Go quickly," he told Kunu. "Find long straight branches and small dead trees. There are many on the ground near the creek. The rest of us will pick up loose bark. Cottonwood bark is thick and strong. We will pile everything here on this level place. We will build our shelter and then go for food. Drink water now. It will help give us strength and energy for our work. Go quickly."

The work took Kunu's mind off his misery. In a short time he was dragging six long branches and two small trees toward the building site. By the time the boy had made three trips, the rest had collected a large pile of bark for the shelter.

Then his grandfather said, "Kunu, we are ready to start building. Help me with the poles. Your mother and sisters are getting more bark."

Hidden under the pile of bark was the axe that Chokay had taken from the wall of the steamboat cabin. Kunu admired the new handle that his grandfather had fashioned from a short piece of cottonwood. The handle was short and thick and now Chokay could put the axe to good use. He cut every pole to the length he decided was correct. After Chokay used strips of hide to tie three poles together near their top ends, Kunu helped him raise the poles up, making a tripod base for their quick shelter. More poles were carefully selected to stand up against the tripod.

Chokay was very happy with the teepee-like frame they had made. He was already laying out slabs of bark for the next step. The deeply grooved pieces of bark were thick and slightly curved. They looked like wooden tiles. Chokay then sent his grandson on another errand: "Kunu, take the axe. Go into the willow bushes. Cut long green stems. Bring them to me."

The boy hurried to the creek, where willow bushes grew ten to twelve feet high. The axe was sharp and worked well. Soon Kunu was back, dragging a large bundle of long willow stems. Chokay immediately started weaving the willow in between the teepee poles. He worked his way around and around, again and again. Each trip around he wove the willows a little higher. The shelter was getting a checkerboard look.

Next Chokay showed Kunu how to stand a row of the thickest bark on the ground by leaning it against the frame. The next row stood on the first one. Rows of bark were laid all the way up the poles, completely covering the frame.

"Kunu, now we need more poles, many of them. Take the axe. Work quickly. Your mother and sisters are standing in the line for food. Darkness is coming soon."

Kunu did work fast. His weariness and hunger would not stop him. As the boy returned with as many long branches as he could drag, Chokay began leaning them against the bark-covered teepee. He explained, "These branches will keep the bark from blowing off our shelter. The nearby trees will help stop the winds. Our shelter is almost finished. My grandson has done his work well."

When darkness came that first night at Crow Creek, Kunu's family gathered into their cozy shelter, more comfortable than most. Kunu's mother and sisters had gathered large bundles of grass and reeds. They laid these on the shelter's floor for a simple mattress to keep everyone off the cold damp ground. It would be much softer and warmer than the bare dirt. Other Winnebago people would crowd into large canvas tents put up by the soldiers. Many would have to sleep in the open.

The food given to the Indian people was a thin soup made from flour, spoiled pork meat and fat, and water. A few stale crackers made this awful soup taste a little better.

In the darkness of their small shelter Chokay spoke to his family. "Each of you has worked hard today. Our journey was hard. We have been cheated out of our homes, our land, and our possessions. We are in a strange land. The soldiers give us spoiled food. Our people are sick. They are hungry. Things will get better. We must stay strong. Tomorrow we will begin work on a new home. Tomorrow we also begin to plan our escape from this place."

9

Working in Secret

Kunu curled up in his blanket. Wakee lay next to him. The boy's first night at Crow Creek was a restless one. First he could not get to sleep. *Begin to plan our escape*—Chokay's words started Kunu's mind racing. Escape? How? When? Who? Where? We have no horse. We have no money. We have no weapon. Chokay cannot walk far. If we are seen, we will be shot. Is escape possible? Chokay, what is your plan? I will help you. I will make you proud, and my father will be proud of his son.

My grandfather will find a way. I, his grandson, will be his legs!

Many more thoughts filled Kunu's mind before he finally drifted off to sleep. His restless dreams were full of confusion. He saw people trying to leave Crow Creek. Their legs moved, but they stayed in the same place. Soldiers were everywhere. Kunu's mother and sisters walked in front of him. He ran but could not catch up with them. The dreams kept coming. Kunu was sweating in his blanket. Then he was damp and cold. His shivering woke him up. He found his blanket at his feet.

In the morning Kunu felt worse than ever. The sour soup he had eaten the night before had made him sick. He ran from the shelter to vomit over and over until his stomach burned with pain. Chokay came to Kunu as he knelt on his hands and knees. The old man placed his wrinkled hand on his grandson's back.

"The food was bad, Kunu. Many others are sick. Today we must boil all our food. We will search the land for roots and berries. We will drink much water. My grandson, we will make ourselves strong. We will build a bigger and better shelter. But remember, we will start now to prepare for our escape."

The days ahead would be horrible for the Winnebago and Sioux people at Crow Creek. The old and the sick grew weaker. Every day someone died. Death songs were heard day and night. Mothers gave birth to babies born dead. Sorrow and grief filled the rows of shelters.

The healthy people planted crops. The best land was near the river and the creek. Corn got a good start before the rain stopped. But then the weather turned hot and dry and all the cornstalks withered and died. Not one ear of corn could be harvested.

Meanwhile, Chokay directed the building of a larger shelter. Kunu and his family worked every day. As soon as the larger home was started, Chokay called Kunu aside. "Grandson, walk with me. We go to the creek bank."

Kunu noticed a serious tone in his grandfather's voice. Although for a while the boy had forgotten about Chokay's talk of escape, in a few minutes escape would become part of Kunu's every thought.

Chokay led his grandson to a large cottonwood tree lying in the dense part of the wooded area. The bark of this dead tree had been used on the new shelter. The trunk was huge. It was twelve feet around at its thickest place. "Kunu, this tree will be used for our escape," Chokay said softly.

The boy stood staring down at the dead giant. He wondered how a fallen tree like this could help. He didn't know it yet, but this tree would become one of the most important things in his young life. He would spend days and weeks with this special tree.

Chokay began to explain his plan. "Kunu, our escape will be made in this tree. The tree will carry us away from this place. It will take the place of my legs. Today you and I begin making our dugout boat. The axe I took from the steamboat will be our main tool. Fire will also be our tool."

A dugout boat to carry us away! Kunu realized that this tree was in Chokay's plan all the time. The boy stood silently, unable to take his eyes off the tree in front of him. Chokay started near the upturned roots. He

paced off six large steps. With the axe the old man marked his stopping place on the trunk.

"This part will be our dugout," said Chokay. "We will work here, unseen, in secret. Each day we will cover our work with many branches. Every chip of wood, we will carry away from this place. No one must see us. When you come here, I must know. When you return, I must know. Our hard work will prepare us for the day of our escape.

"You and I will leave this place in our dugout on the great river. Your mother and sisters will walk in the night with other families. All of us must leave. Already over a hundred of our Winnebago brothers and sisters have died here. Death will overtake all our people if we stay. Our only hope is to leave. Your Chokay needs his grandson to help steer the dugout. We will follow the rivers all the way back to our homeland in Minnesota. There I can die and be buried in the sacred place of my ancestors. There I can join your grandmother in the earth blessed by my fathers and their fathers. Kunu, prepare yourself for our escape!"

Chokay spoke no more about the plan. Instead, he took the short-handled axe and cut some marks on each end of the section to be used for the dugout. When he was finished, Kunu could see the rough outline of the dugout. Then, with a sweep of his arm, Chokay signaled Kunu to follow him home.

The two walked to their shelter in silence. The boy's heart was pounding. Now he knew his grandfather's plan. Escape in a dugout, follow the rivers back to Minnesota. Could it be done? Kunu smiled. If Chokay said it could be done, then it could! Kunu was ready to follow his grandfather anywhere.

Back at their temporary home, Chokay took a sixteen-inch section of cottonwood branch. With his knife Chokay began carving a miniature dugout. While the old man worked, he talked to Kunu. He explained each step that would be used to make the real dugout.

First, the giant log would be cut so it had a long flat surface on its top side and would look like a large bench. Next, a groove would be cut down into the tree from one end of the "bench" to the other. When the groove was several inches deep, dry twigs would be laid in the center of it. Fire would be brought to burn the long line of twigs. More twigs would be added to make the fire burn deeper and deeper into the tree. Water would be poured on the edges to keep the sides from burning. When the fire had burned to a certain depth, it would be put out with water. Next, the axe and the knives would be used to cut and dig out the charred wood.

Chokay said that the last step in making the dugout would be to cut it away from the rest of the tree. Each end of the dugout would be tapered to a point. The front end would be the sharper one. This way the dugout could cut through the water easily.

Every day some work was done on the dugout. Whenever Kunu walked to the dugout to work, Chokay reminded him to go a different way. "That way," Grandfather had explained, "we do not make a path for someone to follow. Also, we will not go at the same time each day. No one must notice what we are doing. When you work, I will watch for trouble for you. When I work, you watch for me. We will keep working often and hard. Soon we will be ready."

Kunu's favorite time was his time to work on the dugout. Each time he went there he could see the boat taking shape. When it was ready for burning, Grandfather had told Kunu he must wait for the wind to blow north and east. This way no smoke would be noticed by the soldiers or anyone else back at the fort.

One day, Kunu was burning the log and the wind was perfect. Suddenly it changed direction! It started blowing the smoke directly back toward the fort. The fire had to be put out fast, but water would just make more smoke. Kunu knew what to do. He did it as fast as he could. Large clumps of sod and dirt lay ready in a pile nearby. Kunu rushed to throw the sod and dirt into the dugout, smothering both the fire and the smoke.

Kunu knew he should tell his grandfather what had happened. It was almost a mile back to the fort. Kunu covered the dugout with a thick layer of branches and then turned and ran through the trees. He jumped the fallen ones. He pushed his way through the willow bushes.

Soon Kunu was close to the edge of the trees. When he stopped at the last second before coming out of the woods, the boy spotted two soldiers walking straight toward him. He had never seen soldiers this far from the fort. Why were they coming this way now? he wondered. They must have seen the smoke. They must know something is happening in the woods. I'm caught. No time to run. I think they see me. What can I do?

The boy had to think fast. He turned and scooped up some dry wood, his hands moving very quickly. As the soldiers came up to the trees, Kunu walked out with all the firewood he could carry. The soldiers stopped. The boy acted as if he did not see them. He walked at a right angle away from the two men.

"Stop!" shouted one of the soldiers. "What are you doing?"

Kunu stopped. He took a deep breath. He gripped the wood tighter so the men would not see his hands shake. He turned slowly to face the two white men. "I am Kunu. My grandfather cannot walk. My mother cares for my young sisters. I gather firewood."

The men seemed to look right into Kunu's head as if to read the thoughts racing through his mind. Do they believe me? Why are they here? What do they know? I'll never show them the dugout. "No matter what they do to me I will never show them where it is hidden," Kunu promised himself silently.

"Have you seen a horse in the trees?" the same soldier asked the boy. "Do you know who stole one of our horses? Someone is planning to escape. Do you know anything about it? If you do, you had better speak up right now!"

The soldier had moved toward Kunu as he spoke. Now the man stood just one step away. "Drop that wood, boy. Look at me. Tell me what you know. If you don't speak up, you'll be in big trouble. Understand?"

"I did not see any horses," Kunu said after he dropped his load of wood. "I will help you find the horse. I can follow the tracks. I will start now."

Kunu's quick thinking and offer to help fooled the soldiers. They never expected an offer to help. The soldier who had not yet spoken told Kunu they did not need his help. "Never mind. We'll find the horse and the one who took it. When we do, all you no-good Indians will see what happens to those who steal horses and try to escape. The lesson you savages learn will never be forgotten."

Without a word, Kunu picked up the wood and headed home. He was still shaking when he dropped his load outside their shelter.

10

A Treasure on the Missouri

Kunu told Chokay the whole frightening story about the change of wind direction, his smothering the fire, and the soldier who stopped him.

Chokay was pleased with Kunu's quick thinking. "My grandson has done well. You used good words to fool the soldiers. The horse they look for is dead. The animal got loose. It stepped in a badger hole and broke its leg. Other soldiers shot it. Our people are already taking the meat for food. It will be much better than the rotten pork."

"Chokay, the dugout is getting deeper and deeper each day. How will we know when to stop the burning? How will we know when the dugout is ready?" The boy was becoming impatient and eager to leave this place.

"Kunu, our time to escape is close. Tomorrow I will go with you. We will work together. Your mother will watch for trouble while we work. We must be leaving soon. Cold weather is coming. The leaves on the trees are even now changing color."

"But Grandfather, when will my mother and sisters escape? How will they travel? And how will we find them after our escape?"

"Kunu, what I tell you now you must keep in your heart," said Chokay very solemnly. "Do not speak about it to anyone. Many of our people are planning to leave this place soon. They will walk the riverbank and will travel together. They will leave one day when darkness comes. They will walk south. There will be so many people leaving at the same time that the white soldiers will not dare shoot them. Your mother and sisters will go with our friends. Everyone will help each other. They will be safe. When your father returns from the war, we will

all get back together again. The army will have to tell
your father where to find his family. Now remember, my
grandson, tell no one anything. Keep the words locked in
your heart. If the soldiers find out, escape for our people
will be impossible. Pray to Earthmaker for all our people
in this time of great danger."

Kunu had watched his grandfather's face as he spoke
each word. The boy was so excited he could hardly keep
from shouting. He knew in his heart that all would go
well. If his Chokay said it was possible, then it was—and
all would go as he said.

The next morning Kunu and Chokay were up at the
first light of day. They slipped into the trees next to Crow
Creek. Kunu could guess that the one-mile walk to the
dugout caused Chokay much pain. But the old man
never stopped. He never complained. Kunu saw his
grandfather limp more and more with each step he took.
The boy's mother would soon be nearby gathering
firewood and standing guard. If anyone came close, she
would make a certain birdcall to warn Kunu and his
grandfather.

Chokay was happy with the work his grandson had done. Only the finishing work was left. Soon the dugout would be ready to launch.

"Kunu, you have done fine work. The burning is completed. Now we will clean up the inside with the axe and our knives. We will make it smooth. Our last job will be on the outside. We must taper the ends to points. Then we will shape the bottom so it is not rounded. The dugout would tip too easily with a round bottom."

Chokay showed Kunu how the last steps in the work should be done. When Grandfather used the axe, the tool did much more work than it did when Kunu used it. Chokay's weathered hands could make the axe cut perfectly and very fast.

Chokay stopped once to explain the escape plan. "Kunu, when we leave in our dugout, the first miles will be the most dangerous. We must not have even a small accident. There will be no time to stop for anything. We will be the first ones to escape from here. If the wrong soldier sees us, he will shoot and warn the others.

"My grandson has strong legs. Run along the river each day. Study the current. Look for sandbars, rocks, and snags. Pick the safest way for our dugout to go. Put each thing in your mind. When we leave here, you will show your grandfather the best way. We cannot make a mistake."

Kunu's heart beat faster and faster as Chokay spoke. His throat became dry. Grandfather was giving him the most important job of his young life. "Study the river. Pick the way. We must be right," he told himself. The boy knew Grandfather was putting their lives in his hands. Kunu told himself he could do it. He would do it. He *must* do it!

The boy's first run along the Missouri River was only half a mile. In that short distance he saw many problems. There were two large sandbars. Each one had dead trees sticking out of the sand and partly blocking the channels around them. All along that half a mile, the current moved from one side to the other.

Kunu also saw lots of places where rocks lay in the river. Some rocks were hard to see in the muddy water, even those just below the surface. The boy learned to read the ripples where water passed over rocks. In several places large trees lay in the water. Their roots were

upstream and made them easy to see. The most dangerous snags were those just under the surface of the river.
These could cause the dugout to flip right over. After
that first run down the river, Kunu knew why Chokay
wanted him to study the river. He also knew why Grandfather wanted him to go many times. There was much to
remember. The boy had seen only a short stretch of the
river, but he now understood how tricky the river would
be. And they would have to travel hundreds and hundreds of miles on it! This would be an unbelievable
escape on the Missouri river, but he knew it would happen as Chokay had said.

On Kunu's third trip down the riverbank he made an
exciting discovery. He had stopped to look at a large logjam that blocked a fast-moving channel. The water was
running right under the huge pile of logs and into a quiet
pool below. In the pile of logs Kunu's keen eyes saw an
unusual shape that he knew was not just another piece
of driftwood. It was different. He sensed it would be a
great discovery. The shape the boy spotted looked like
the end of an oar. When he looked closer, Kunu knew it
was an oar. It had probably washed off a boat some-

where upstream and had drifted this far before getting stuck in the big logjam.

Kunu knew he had made a wonderful find. Now he had to find a way to get the oar out of the log pile and onto shore. Then he would hide it in a safe place and go tell Chokay the good news. Grandfather would know what to do next.

To get out to the logjam Kunu had to wade through deep mud, cross a place where the current was swift, and finally pull himself onto the pile of logs. The excited boy remembered to pick up a sturdy pole he could use to keep his balance in the powerful current.

At first, Kunu's feet were sucked into the thick mud, but he pulled hard to get each foot free of the gooey stuff. After the mud came the fast water. Kunu dug the pole in the riverbed and braced himself against the strong current. Twice he almost got swept away. Six feet from the logjam, Kunu suddenly found himself in very deep water. The muddy water had hidden this hole well. The boy dropped all the way under, but he let his feet touch bottom and then pushed upward with all his strength. Kunu broke above the surface in time to grab a thick branch sticking out of the pile of logs. Using all his pulling power, he got close enough to raise one leg over a large log. The rest seemed easy.

Kunu wasted no time in climbing over the logjam to the other side. There was the oar, right in front of him! Kunu hoped the oar would be good enough to serve as a paddle for the dugout. He couldn't tell that yet, because he could only see part of the oar. It has to be good, the boy thought. He knew Chokay would be proud of him when he saw what he found. Kunu was anxious to pry the oar out and get going back to his grandfather.

If would be a while before Kunu would know how good his discovery really was. The oar was held in the pile by the weight of many logs. In fact, it would take the boy more than an hour to loosen the oar enough to pull it from the pile.

Kunu worked hard until he had the oar halfway out. Suddenly he had to stop working and scramble into the logjam to hide. His first sign of trouble had been the sound of a horse whinnying. With a turn of his head, he had caught the sight of four soldiers on horseback coming down the riverbank right toward him. Kunu struggled

into a position to hide himself in the maze of logs. He scratched himself across the back and hit his head on a log as he wiggled his way into the pile.

Although Kunu was out of sight, he could see the soldiers. They must be looking for me, he thought. Why else would they be here right now? In all his other trips down the river, he had seen no one. Kunu studied the men closely. They were not looking at the ground. Maybe they had not seen his tracks. Also, the white soldiers were talking and not paying close attention to anything around them.

The hidden boy did not take his eyes off the men. Soon they were close enough so he could hear every word they were saying. Kunu could see the expressions on their faces and felt sure they did not know he was there. He hoped they would not see his tracks in the mud. Anyway, since the mud did not hold a clear track, maybe they would think an animal made them.

The men passed by without even looking Kunu's way. He did not dare come out until he was sure they were far enough away not to see him. When Kunu got back to work, the oar slowly began to loosen more. In a few minutes the boy would know whether the oar was any good. He was getting more and more excited every minute.

Kunu could not believe his eyes. One last pull and the oar came out, and it was perfect. There was not a single crack in it. The boy felt like shouting for joy. He was so happy that his whole body tingled. He could scarcely wait to get back to Chokay with the great news.

11

One More Night

Kunu knew his next problem was getting the oar to shore safely. He did not want to lose it in the river. Once on shore he would then have to find a good hiding place for this treasure. Hiding an oar this long would not be easy.

Kunu used the oar to make his way through the swift current. He held on to it with all his strength. Near shore, the boy followed his own tracks through the deep mud and reached solid ground. Kunu looked in every direction. He did not want anyone to see him, so he stayed

121

partially hidden in the willow bushes and high reeds growing on the river bottom and nearby.

Carefully Kunu searched for a good hiding place for the oar, which was eight feet long and would not be easy to hide. The boy worked his way through the dense brush. At the edge of a clump of bushes, Kunu found the perfect spot to hide his treasure. In fact he fell over the hiding place. A long log lay well hidden by tall grass. It had obviously been washed up on the bank during high water, years ago. Kunu knew this was a perfect location. He quickly slid the oar into the grass and then pushed it along the ground next to the log. It went into the thick grass and was soon out of sight. The oar was completely hidden alongside the log. No one would see any sign of it, Kunu was certain.

Kunu made sure that he would remember this place. A large dead cottonwood tree stood only thirty feet away. Its bare branches stood outlined like a skeleton against the sky. When Kunu left the scene and headed home, he stopped often to look back at the big dead tree. He memorized the view so well that he knew he could find the oar's hiding place, even in the dark.

Chokay was very happy to hear the good news about the oar. "Kunu, Earthmaker is helping us. He knows his people need him. The Great Spirit has given you the gift of the oar. He protected you from the soldiers. He did not let their eyes see you. Our escape begins soon. Come with me. I have something for my grandson to see."

Chokay led Kunu into their bark-covered house. The old man dropped to his knees and with both hands pushed the grass back off one part of the floor. Hidden under the grass was a long piece of cottonwood. One end was a part of the root system and was very thick. Kunu saw how Chokay had flattened the thick end so it could be used as a strong paddle or a pole for pushing off the riverbed.

Grandson, I was going to start making another paddle today," said Chokay. "Instead I will finish the dugout. Since we have two good paddles, we can leave one day earlier. There will be no moon tonight. When darkness comes and the night is old, you must go to the hiding place. Get the oar. Follow the river. Stay in the bushes and trees and listen for the soldiers. Bring the oar here to our shelter. I will be waiting for you."

Darkness came to Fort Thompson. As people prepared for sleep, they covered their fires with dirt and sod to keep the coals hot until morning. The only sounds in the Winnebago camp that dark night were made by a family singing a death song for their four-year-old daughter, who had died that day. Kunu's heart was heavy with sadness for the family. In the past two months he had seen many of his people die. There was barely enough food to keep the Indians alive. Suffering and sadness filled the camp each passing day.

"Kunu, go now. Go quickly. Go safely. Return soon. I will be ready for you," whispered Chokay. Kunu was glad to be out and moving. He had sat in the darkness a long time, waiting for his grandfather to send him out.

The boy strained to see where to put his feet. Although his eyes were used to the dark, rocks, roots, and holes in the ground were still hard to see. Kunu lifted his feet high to keep from stumbling over anything. He was able to keep his balance when he stepped on uneven ground. The trip down the river took twenty-five minutes. Kunu was glad to see the giant cottonwood with its bare branches reaching high above the ground.

Kunu walked from the big tree straight toward the river. He had no trouble finding the grass-covered log. His hands felt through the grass to the oar. It was right where he had left it. Kunu felt a sense of great relief. The boy pulled the oar out and headed for home.

The closer Kunu got to the fort, the more excited he became. All was still in the fort. The boy heard no sounds anywhere. Only one oil lamp burned in an army building in the fort. Kunu moved quickly. He passed several shelters and disappeared into his own home. He had made it. The oar was safely home.

Chokay was waiting. He had a small fire burning in the fire pit on the floor in the center of the one-room shelter. Kunu's mother and sisters were sitting up to see it all. Grandfather was very pleased to see the oar. It was even better than he thought it would be. Since the oar was made of hardwood, it would be very strong. Quietly and carefully Chokay measured the beautiful oar. He put a mark on it and began cutting.

Chokay explained what would happen next. "The oar must be shortened. I am cutting it so you can use it as your paddle. I will use the one I made of cottonwood. Tomorrow we will get everything ready to leave. Many other people are planning their escape. Others are out looking for trees for making dugouts. Hundreds of Chief Winneshiek's people are getting ready to walk south on the riverbank. Kunu, we will be the first to escape. We are ready."

Kunu sat silently listening to his grandfather speak as he worked. He watched Chokay's gnarled hands use the knife to cut skillfully through the hardwood. Grandfather's hands and arms were powerful. In a short time the handle was cut in two. Chokay carefully rounded the end of the shortened paddle so it would fit Kunu's hand just right.

Chokay motioned to Kunu to pick up the end of the oar that had been cut off. "Take this piece. And take the wood shavings. Go to the river. Put them in the current where the river will carry all of it away."

Kunu made a fast trip to the river. When he returned, Chokay was in his bed. The boy rolled up in his blankets and tried to get comfortable. "Try to sleep," whispered Chokay. "Our paddles are made. Our dugout is ready. Your mother and sisters have a bag of food saved for us. After this night and one more we will make our escape."

Kunu was tired, but it took him more than an hour to fall asleep. Dreams came and went. When morning came, the boy felt tired and sore. The day was cloudy and cold. By the white man's calendar, it was September 29, 1863.

Summer was over. Winter would come soon. Before the coming winter would end, hundreds of Winnebago people at Fort Thompson would die. Hundreds of others would leave before December. Kunu and Chokay would be two of the first to attempt an escape. Being first would make their escape very dangerous. Their big day would come on September 30, 1863.

Chokay and Kunu made one trip to their dugout that final day at Fort Thompson. It was ready. They pulled the dugout through the trees to the edge of Crow Creek. Grandfather had a place all picked out where the dugout could be hidden. The next day they would put their belongings into the dugout. A large buffalo hide without its fur would serve as a pack. With everything wrapped

in the large hide, it could be tied into the dugout. Chokay had made two holes on each side of the dugout near the top edges. Strips of hide would be pulled through the holes and used for ties.

On the way back to their shelter, Kunu had a big question for his grandfather. It had been bothering the boy since he heard Chokay say they would leave in daylight. "Chokay, if we leave in the daytime, the soldiers can see us. Shouldn't we leave at night?"

"Kunu, I have been watching the soldiers every day. Most of them are building places to live this winter. They work all morning until the bugle calls them to eat their noon meal. Then no soldiers are on guard near the river. That is when we will leave. If someone is watching, I have a plan that will keep us hidden. One day I stood on the riverbank and saw a tree floating by. Its branches still had many leaves. When we float by in our dugout, we will have leaves on *our* branches too."

"Chokay, our dugout has no branches," Kunu reminded the old man.

"Wait, grandson. Listen to your grandfather. We will have branches and leaves. Before we enter the river, we will cut a live tree. We will lay it over our dugout with its branches and leaves hiding us. When we float past the fort, we will look like just another tree going downriver. Only when we are safely away from the fort will we throw the tree into the water."

Chokay's words painted a clear picture in Kunu's mind. The boy could see a tree floating past the fort. He saw Chokay and himself hidden from view beneath the branches and leaves. The river was more than half a mile wide. No one would notice the hidden dugout if it went down the middle of the river far from shore.

"Kunu, many people go to the trees every day, looking for logs to make into dugouts. We will not wait until tomorrow to pack our things into the boat. Tonight we will do that work. Then you must stay with the dugout all night. Sleep in the boat. Tomorrow I will come with our axe. When the soldiers are called to eat, we will slide our dugout into the creek and leave. Before we enter the river, I will cut a tree to cover us. I have one picked out."

Chokay had thought of everything. Kunu's mind was racing over and over with the words his grandfather had just spoken. The boy knew the plan was good. He was more excited than he had ever been in his young life.

Later that day Kunu realized he would have to say goodbye to his mother and his sisters that night. He would ask Earthmaker to walk with them, to guide their feet, and to lead them safely away from this place of misery and death. The boy had not asked Chokay about his dog, but he knew that Wakee would have to stay with Kunu's mother and sisters. The dugout would be no place for a dog, so he would have to say good-bye to Wakee, too.

All this was hard for a ten-year-old boy to understand in such a short time. He loved his family very much. He missed his father more than ever. If his father were here, he knew his mother and sisters would be safe.

Chokay kept telling Kunu that everything would be all right. Grandfather had fasted often, asking Earthmaker to protect all of his Winnebago children, young and old. Grandfather was full of wisdom and strength, so the boy trusted Chokay's words. Yes, somehow everything would be all right. Grandfather said that one day his father would return from the war. He would find his family and would bring everyone together. Life would be good again.

Kunu would also ask Earthmaker for help. He would pray to the Great Spirit to make him brave and strong so he would be able to do everything Chokay asked him to do.

12

A Risky Escape

The night of September 29 was quite warm. The dugout was already loaded with most of the things Chokay and Kunu would take. Kunu sat in his Crow Creek home for the last time and rubbed Wakee's ears. His mother and little sisters sat on their blankets. No one spoke.

Finally Chokay came in and took his seat. "Kunu, it is time for you to go to the dugout. Go quietly and carefully. The night will pass. I will come at daylight. All morning we will rest. When the sun is high and the soldiers eat, we will begin our journey."

Kunu's mother stared at her son. Her eyes were red from many tears and her face showed how tired she was. Often Kunu had seen his mother give up her own food so Henu and Wehuh would have enough to eat. He had watched his mother come home many times with roots and berries. He knew she had gone far from the fort to find them. People had already gathered all the wild food that grew nearby.

How Kunu's heart ached for his family and his dog. Leaving them was the hardest thing he had ever had to do. The boy held his grandfather's words in his heart: "Earthmaker will travel with all his children. He will help us."

Kunu threw his arms around his sisters' necks. He told them to be strong and brave. He told them to help their mother and that Earthmaker would bring them all back together soon. Winnebago Indian boys never hugged their sisters. They never showed their feelings. But now it was different. Kunu knew that these few minutes were not like any other time in his life.

The boy's mother hugged him and whispered some special words to him. Then she reached for a bag made of deerhide. She had decorated it with beads from her own clothes. Inside the bag were some small cakes baked with delicious berries in the center. Also inside was some sugar that Kunu's mother had been saving for a special occasion. The sugar was in hard lumps and wrapped in cloth. The boy would open the bag later and find these wonderful things. He would be reminded once again of the special love his mother had for her son.

Kunu walked from the shelter with a heavy heart and a hollow weakness in his legs. He felt loneliness like he had never experienced before. Although he was tempted to go back and see his mother and sisters just once more, he knew he could not. Chokay was counting on him to do his part and to be brave. There was no turning back. Kunu walked on through the darkness alone.

The boy's night in the dugout went slowly. He did sleep about half the time, but night sounds woke him up often. The cries of a nighthawk, an owl, and several coyotes were the only sounds of life he heard in the darkness.

Chokay came at daylight as he had promised. The morning passed even slower than the night had. Finally, when the sun was high, Kunu and Chokay pulled the loaded dugout from the willow bushes. The creek was shallow, and Grandfather had picked a place where the water stood in a pool three feet deep. Here they slid the dugout into the water for the first time. Kunu was excited to see it float at last. It looked beautiful. The boy was proud, since he had built much of it. Soon it would carry them down the great river and away from the place he hated so deeply.

Chokay motioned to Kunu to climb into the front section. As the boy put his weight on the dugout, he could tell that it was strong. He also knew that it could tip if he and his grandfather did not balance it well. Chokay was in right after Kunu. With their paddles, they took their first strokes. The boy watched the dugout make its first few feet through the water. He realized that the thick sides would be much better than the bark canoes other Indian people used on quieter streams and lakes.

After moving in silence for some time, Chokay said, "Grandson, we stop here. Hold the dugout next to the bank."

Chokay slid over the back of the boat and stepped onto a rock. From there he crossed to the creek bank and went right to work on a small tree. Every stroke of the axe hit its mark. The tree came down smoothly and quietly. Grandfather trimmed a few branches and dragged the tree to the bank next to the dugout.

"Kunu, pull on the branches. The top of the tree must hang over the front of the boat. The trunk will go over the back. I made the cut so it looks as if a beaver did the work." With the tree covering the dugout, everything was ready for the river trip to begin. But it would be a dangerous beginning.

The current when they entered the river would be perfect, they knew. It would carry the dugout away from the eastern shore and out to the middle of the river. Kunu stood in the shallow water of Crow Creek. He held the dugout and waited. Chokay sat in the boat, waiting and listening, too.

Kunu was so excited he could hardly stand still. Waiting was hard. Come on, blow that bugle, thought Kunu. For the soldiers, the bugle would be the signal to come to eat. For Chokay and Kunu, the bugle would be the signal for escape.

When the bugle did sound the call, Kunu could barely hear it because a steady breeze carried the sound in the other direction. But he did hear it, and so did Chokay. The boy climbed into the dugout between the branches that would hide him from view. Chokay used his sturdy paddle to push off against the creek bottom. His strong arms and shoulders gave the dugout a boost with every push. The camouflaged boat slid into the great Missouri River with ease.

Kunu crouched forward over the front of the dugout, his head between the trunk of the tree and one of its branches. He could look through the leaves and see the shoreline. There were the first few buildings of the fort. Kunu's eyes searched for soldiers. There were none to be seen. It's working, he realized. Chokay has picked the perfect time to leave. Soon we'll be away from the soldiers and the fort. We have fooled them! We will not get

shot! These thoughts made Kunu feel happier than he had felt in months.

The dugout floated peacefully along. It was slowly drifting at an angle away from the fort. The current carried it to the center of the river and on downstream. Kunu's thoughts turned to his father, his mother, his sisters, and his dog—Earthmaker is with us today. He will be with us every day. Chokay and I will return to Minnesota. Father will find all of us. He will bring us together, as Chokay said it would be. My Chokay has great wisdom and will always find a way!—The boy had these wonderful thoughts as the dugout drifted farther and farther from the fort. The breeze continued. It was ruffling the leaves on the tree that disguised the small craft.

Kunu was getting stiff from kneeling in the same position so long. He moved back a little and realized that his neck was sore. He had kept his eyes on the eastern shore the whole time. Now the fort was far behind. The boy relaxed a little as he changed positions. Kunu bumped his head on a branch but finally found a good place to sit. He took his first look at the other side of the river. He was surprised to see how close they had come to the west bank. The bank was steep, at least twenty feet high. The river's current had cut the bank away. The same current had carried the dugout to this side of the river.

Kunu looked closely at the bank. Roots of trees hung out near the top. A few trees had toppled halfway over, with their branches hanging down toward the water. The boy wondered when Chokay would say they could throw the tree they were carrying overboard. He would be glad to get rid of it. Not only would it be easier to see, but they could go faster if they paddled. They could also steer better and be able to follow the fastest part of the river. Kunu was anxious to get rid of the tree.

This was another time Chokay was wiser than his grandson. As they were passing the high bank, Kunu saw a movement behind a tree standing near the edge. After the dugout floated a little farther, Kunu saw something that made him hold his breath. Just when he had thought they were safe, there it was—the enemy armed and ready to shoot them on sight! Not a hundred feet away, a soldier sat mounted on his horse. He was facing the river. The boy was sure the man was looking right at the dugout. Can he see us? Will he shoot? Does Chokay see the soldier?

Kunu watched the soldier's every move. When they were even with the man, he jumped from his horse. The soldier tied the animal to a tree and then pulled his rifle from its holder on the saddle. The white man took three quick steps and knelt down on one knee next to a tree. He was still looking right at the dugout. The boy wanted to tell Chokay they had been seen. Should they jump into the water? he wondered. They could hang on to the dugout and could keep the boat between them and the soldier. No bullet could go through the dugout.

"I see him," whispered Chokay. "Don't move. Look the other way."

Kunu was confused. Why did Chokay want him to look the other way? Before the boy could turn his head far enough to see anything in the other direction, he heard something splash. There in the water was the answer. A deer was swimming across the river. It was going to pass right in front of the dugout.

"Kunu, the soldier watches the deer. Don't make a sound," Chokay said softly.

The boy watched the deer pass in front of the dugout only forty feet away. Suddenly the animal caught the scent of humans close by. The breeze had carried Kunu's odor to the deer. The animal's ears went up. Its nose tested the air. In an instant the deer changed direction and began swimming downstream. Kunu saw the soldier jump up. The man started running along the bank just out of sight of the animal.

Only the deer's head was above water. A sandbar was right in front of it. As soon as the deer's feet hit the bottom, it started across the sandbar and headed for deeper water. Shore was only a short distance from the sandbar. Once ashore, the deer's speed would carry it to safety. As the deer's body came out of the water, the soldier moved to the edge of the riverbank. He went down on one knee. The deer saw him and tried to hurry over the sandbar and head back across the river the way it had come. The deer could not move fast enough. The soldier fired. The deer was hit, but the wounded animal was able to get off the sandbar and into the deeper

water. The soldier fired again. This bullet hit the water a
foot from the fleeing animal.

The soldier watched as the animal swam away. Its
head went under several times. The deer was getting
weaker and weaker. The white man followed along the
bank for a short time. He stopped and took one last shot.
When he missed again, he turned to walk back to his
horse.

Kunu had watched it all. He knew it had been a narrow escape. If they had jumped into the water, the soldier would have seen them. Now the boy could watch
the enemy ride on north and leave the deer to die in the
river. What had been a close call would now become a
great gift.

Chokay said quietly, "Kunu, put your paddle in the
water on the side of the dugout toward the middle of the
river. Hold it out from the boat. It will help us turn
toward the deer. Keep your eyes on the animal. The
enemy has given us meat."

13

Overboard!

The chase was on. It was a strange scene. A struggling animal was being followed by a floating tree that seemed to be talking.

"Kunu, get down low. Lie on your back. Put your feet against the tree above you. Find a place where your feet can push on the trunk. When I say your name, push the tree up as high as you can."

It happened smoothly. Kunu pushed with his feet as Grandfather lifted his own end of the tree and rolled it over into the river. The boy watched as it floated free.

"Paddle! Paddle!" called Chokay. "The soldier is gone. We must catch the deer!"

It felt good to sit up straight again. Kunu dug his paddle into the water. Grandfather headed the boat right at the deer. The wounded animal was so weak that its head was staying under longer and longer. The boy was surprised at the struggle the deer made to keep going. Whenever it seemed the animal could not go another minute, it would suddenly fight even harder to get away. Finally the deer hit the roots of a large tree sticking above the water. Here it gave up its fight and died.

Chokay aimed for the upended tree. When the dugout was fifteen feet from the roots, Chokay told Kunu to put his paddle in the water on the left side. The boy knew to hold it straight out next to the front of the boat. This helped turn the dugout left. Chokay paddled on the right. When the dugout came up to the roots, Grandfather jumped into the water and grabbed the dead deer by one leg. With all his strength, Chokay rolled the animal into the dugout. At the same time Kunu was paddling forward, so only the back of the dugout brushed against the roots. Grandfather had gotten out of the way

before he could be trapped between the boat and the half-submerged tree. The current caused the dugout to slide past the roots. When Chokay saw his chance, he pulled himself up and over the back point of the dugout to safety.

"Kunu, paddle for shore. We'll head for those bushes. They will hide us."

A small inlet allowed Chokay to steer the dugout into the bushes and out of sight. Kunu held the boat steady while Chokay pulled the deer to shore. Without a word, his grandfather began cleaning the deer. He worked fast. Chokay had the animal skinned and the best meat cut from the bones in record time. He used the hide to wrap the meat securely.

Kunu had not seen fresh meat for a long time, but he had not watched the cleaning and cutting. Instead, Chokay had sent him out to the edge of the bushes to stand guard. His grandfather called him back in time to see the meat being wrapped in the hide. "We have received a great gift from Earthmaker," said Chokay. "Tonight we will eat fresh meat. We will cook all the meat so it will not spoil so fast. I wish we could take some to your mother and little sisters, but it is too dangerous to try."

Kunu stood ready to push the dugout back into the river. He said nothing. Once again in his mind he could see his mother, tired and weak, handing him a bag of her food. Now he and Chokay had delicious meat. The boy longed to run back up the river to give her his share of this meat. It was hard just to leave and not be able to share this great gift with those he loved so much.

Once more Chokay was in the dugout. Kunu waded next to the boat, pushing it into deeper water. Then the boy came over the high front end head first. With a smooth move he took his seat and began paddling. Before long, Kunu would be an expert with his paddle. His arms would grow stronger every day. Hundreds of miles of river were ahead of the two travelers, but this first day was a good beginning.

The roasted deer meat was the best Kunu had ever tasted. Chokay had started the fire with a spark from his piece of flint. They had hidden the dugout safely in the reeds growing along the river bank. While they ate, Chokay cut the rest of the meat into thin strips. He showed Kunu how to make a rack out of willow branches. The green willow stems were woven loosely in a checkerboard pattern. Two branches were driven into the ground with forked ends up. The rack was held over the fire as it rested on the forked ends.

Chokay told Kunu to keep feeding the fire. Grandfather was kept busy covering the rack with strips of meat. He turned them over a few times while they cooked. When a batch was cooked all the way through, it was removed. Batch after batch, Chokay cooked all the meat and laid it out on the deer hide to cool.

The night seemed short. There was a clear sky in the morning. The buffalo hide had served as a bed, and their blankets had kept them warm. Kunu woke up with a sharp pain in his stomach. He had eaten too much meat. His stomach was not used to such rich food. "You will feel better soon," Chokay said. "The sun will come over the river before long. We must be on our way. The fort is still close."

The boy helped his grandfather fold the buffalo hide into a tight pack. Chokay tied it into the dugout. The deer hide full of the cooled meat was placed under the pack where the sun could not reach it. It would stay cool there. Soon Kunu did forget about his stomach.

The dugout was in the river only a short time when there was trouble and the boy did not see it coming. Before Kunu knew what was happening, the dugout had struck a solid snag. It turned the boat to the side so fast that Kunu lost his balance and rolled overboard. Chokay saw what was happening in time to jump out on the opposite side. The old man caught the edge of the dugout and kept it from going all the way over. Kunu had gone all the way under. He came up too fast and bumped his head on the boat floating over him. Then the boy opened his eyes in time to see his paddle heading downstream.

"Inside, Kunu! Get back in the boat! Hurry!" called Grandfather.

Chokay was at the very back of the dugout, holding it steady as it pulled him along. Kunu grabbed the side of the boat and hand-over-hand worked his way to the front. It took all his strength to raise himself onto the bow. The boy was soaked and had swallowed some of the muddy water. Kunu coughed and spit out as much of it as he could. He dropped into his seat and caught his breath.

Chokay followed Kunu into the boat. He grabbed his paddle and began his powerful strokes again. "Kunu, be ready! When we come up to your paddle, get it! Don't miss."

The boy felt helpless. His grandfather was doing all the work. All Kunu could do was sit and wait. There was his paddle coasting along ahead of the dugout. Chokay was gaining on it. Kunu leaned forward as far as he dared. Chokay put the boat right next to the paddle. One grab and the boy pulled it in. He felt so good when he dipped the blade in the water and took the first stroke.

"My eyes did not see the snag, Chokay. I will watch with better eyes," Kunu promised.

"My grandson has done well. We will be ready for more danger. The river hides many things from us. You listened well. We will help each other. Together we will make it down this great river. We will not let it stop us."

Kunu strained his eyes as he searched every inch of the water ahead. He told his grandfather about every little ripple that might be the sign of a hidden rock or snag.

Seeing the trouble spots in time would make it possible to avoid them. Chokay saw that the boy would become good at "reading" the river before long.

There were several close calls during the next two days. Kunu's warnings were always in time for Chokay's paddle to guide the dugout safely around each trouble spot. Grandfather told the boy there would be a time soon when they would cut another tree to hide their boat as it floated by a dangerous place. "Fort Randall has many soldiers," he explained. "We will pass it soon. These soldiers will not shoot us, but they might stop us. They might take us back to Fort Thompson. We will float past this fort hidden by another tree."

Chokay had memorized landmarks on the Missouri River as he rode the steamboat to Crow Creek. He had especially watched for places like Fort Randall. Chokay knew where the current was best for taking them past the fort. He had a route picked out that would let them go past far from the sight of anyone near the fort.

Several miles above Fort Randall, Chokay pulled the dugout to the riverbank. A stand of trees grew a short distance from the water. Grandfather cut one of the smaller trees and dragged it to the dugout. It covered the boat even better than the first one had.

There were people on the riverbank near Fort Randall when the dugout floated past in broad daylight. No one even looked twice. Soon the fort was far behind and the tree tossed over the side.

"Chokay, it worked again. No one sees us. We are going to make it," said Kunu confidently.

"Grandson, we will succeed. I know we will. But we must be ready for trouble every minute."

Kunu thought nothing could stop them now. Chokay was too wise and too strong to let anything block their way. The boy had no way of knowing the great danger that was waiting for them only a short distance downstream.

14

Kunu's Bravery

The river below Fort Randall turned a little more east with every mile traveled. Several days passed with nothing to bother Kunu and Chokay. They enjoyed a little meat each day and ate from their small supply of roots and berries, still left from Crow Creek. Kunu shared his mother's special berry cakes and sugar with his grandfather. At their campsite on the sixth night, Kunu listened to Chokay talk about the future.

"Kunu, some of our people never came to Crow Creek. They escaped to Wisconsin, where friendly white people let them live on their land. These good whites protected their Indian brothers and sisters from any harm. We, too, have a white friend. I know Karl's uncle will help us find a place to live. He spoke from his heart when he came for Karl. He said he would help us if we ever needed him. We will return to Minnesota and find him."

"Chokay, how will we get there?" wondered the boy. "Angry white people are everywhere near Karl's home."

"Grandson, we will find a way. By the time we get that far, we will have a plan. Each day that passes brings us closer."

Ahead lay miles and miles of river. The great Missouri River flowed past many settlements that would someday become great cities. Sioux City, Omaha, Council Bluffs, St. Joseph, Kansas City, and St. Louis—all seemed to lie waiting for the tiny boat to go by them. At St. Louis, Kunu and Chokay would leave the Missouri and head up the mighty Mississippi, the largest river of all.

"Kunu, we have far to go. We cannot relax. We must never stop watching for danger," warned the wise old Winnebago. Sure enough, that very day an unseen hazard waited to trap them in its powerful clutches. Soon

Kunu would need to think and act fast to save his grand-father, the dugout, and himself.

It all happened without warning, where the river split into two separate channels. An island divided the river, and Chokay guided the dugout into the right-hand chan-nel. The water began moving faster. There was a rapids ahead. Kunu could hear it. He did not see any dangerous rocks or snags in the rapids, although he watched for them carefully.

The closer the dugout got to the rapids, the louder the water became. Why was this rapids so loud? They didn't seem that strong to the boy. Suddenly Kunu saw what was making the noise. Right ahead of the dugout, the water poured over a shelf of hard clay. The water dropped four feet all at once. It was too late to keep from going over the drop.

"Chokay! The water drops fast!" the boy shouted.

"Hang on, Kunu! Stay with the boat!"

Kunu watched as the nose of the dugout hung over the edge for a split second and then dropped steeply into the boiling water. Before the boy knew it, the whole dugout was full of water. He sat in the boat full of water,

hanging on to his paddle and using it to brace himself against the current that tried to sweep him overboard.

When his eyes cleared, Kunu turned his head. The sight filled him with terror. Chokay was gone! The boy could not see his grandfather anywhere. The dugout was being held in the grip of the boiling water. Tons of water poured over the ledge and into the spot in the boat where Chokay had been sitting.

"Chokay! Chokay!" screamed Kunu. "Where are you? Chokay! Come back!"

Kunu was panicking, but he told himself to keep calm. He had to do something fast. The boat had not moved. Where was Chokay? Had the water swept him away? Was it holding him under to drown?

Holding his paddle across the dugout for balance, Kunu worked his way through the water-filled boat to the back end. From there the boy spotted Chokay, whose head was barely above water. He had been swept overboard into the boiling river. Grandfather kept going under and bobbing back up. Chokay was fighting the water with his arms, but his legs were too weak to help him much. Kunu saw that his grandfather could not last much longer against the power of the water.

The boy had slid all the way to the back and was being hit by the water cascading over the ledge. He anchored his feet under the baggage. Next he took his paddle at one end, leaned over toward Chokay, and held the other end out to him. The struggling man did not see it at first. Kunu reached it a little farther and was almost swept overboard himself. Then Chokay's hand hit the paddle. He could reach it with the fingers of his left hand. Twice his fingers came loose, and he disappeared from sight the second time that he lost his hold.

Under the water, Chokay used his weak legs to push off the bottom of the river and move a little closer to the paddle. As Chokay came out of the water, he quickly grabbed the paddle and held on with both hands. Kunu had never held anything as tightly as he held that paddle. He seemed to have twice his normal strength. With every bit of this strength he pulled back on the paddle. Slowly the boy moved his grandfather a few inches closer to the dugout.

Kunu didn't know what to do next. But Chokay did, and Kunu seemed to be able to read his grandfather's mind. The boy stopped pulling and hung on. With a quick motion he leaned toward Chokay. Instantly his grandfather moved his hands farther up the paddle. Now he had a firm grip with both hands. Kunu had all he could do to just hold on to the paddle. Although the strain on his hands and arms was painful, the boy paid no attention to his pain. This was a battle to save the grandfather he loved with his whole heart.

Chokay's head stayed above water, and he could breathe freely now. This gave his arms the strength they needed. Grandfather started a hand-over-hand climb up the paddle to the dugout. Kunu watched him get closer and closer. Chokay was straddling the paddle to give him better balance against the water. Grandfather concentrated on reaching the edge of the boat. With one final quick move, he gripped the boat with his right hand. Then he rolled over the paddle and caught hold of the dugout with his left hand, too. With the little strength he had left, Chokay pulled himself from the boiling water and dropped into the dugout next to Kunu.

"Kunu, the paddle!" shouted the exhausted Chokay. "I need it. Hang on to the dugout and jump into the water. Put your feet against the bank and push us free. I'll push with the paddle. Go!"

In seconds the boy was in the churning water. He kept a tight grip on the dugout. Kunu looked up at his grandfather. Chokay smiled his encouragement, as only he could at a time like this. The boy knew Chokay was counting on him. Kunu managed to smile back.

Taking a deep breath, the boy went under. When his feet touched bottom, Kunu stretched out, letting his feet find the clay bank. As the dugout rocked back toward the bank a little, Kunu let his knees bend. Before the dugout could move forward, he pushed off with all his strength. The boat barely moved. The boy's head broke the water. His lungs filled with fresh air.

"Once more!" shouted Chokay.

This time Kunu went under as the dugout rocked back toward the bank. He didn't let his feet touch bottom. Instead, he put them against the bank, bent and locked his knees, and with all his strength pushed off, with his shoulder against the dugout.

It was all over in seconds. The dugout seemed to pop out of the boil and pull away. Kunu hung on, while Chokay used his paddle to push the swamped dugout toward the shore. "Kunu, the rapids are shallow! Push toward the bank!"

The tired boy could stand up in the shallow rapids, so he pushed while his grandfather used the paddle as a pole. Near the shore the water swirled gently in a quiet eddy. What a relief it was to be out of the furious rapids. Kunu's arms felt heavy and useless. His legs were wobbly as he turned to listen to his grandfather. "The river surprised us, Kunu. When we came this way by steamboat, there was no drop-off here. The water has gone down. The river has changed."

Chokay looked exhausted. The water had taken his strength, but still Kunu's grandfather went to work. "We must drain the water from the dugout, my grandson," he said. "My paddle is gone. We will find a campsite. Our blankets are wet, and the night will be cold. We have much to do. The weather can end our life, as the water has already tried to do."

Kunu was worn out, but he still worked for several more hours. First, the dugout was pulled to shore and tipped on its side to drain. Then Chokay used Kunu's paddle to guide the boat another mile. In a thick stand of trees Grandfather found a small clearing and built a fire. The wet blankets were wrung out and hung on poles near the fire. Nearby, the buffalo hide was draped from a low hanging branch of a tree.

Chokay made another rack for drying the water-soaked deer meat. He knew that the steady wind would make the cold night seem even colder. "We will sit close to our fire until our blankets are dry. We must eat a good meal. Our bodies are tired and cold. Some of our people have died in their sleep when they were wet and cold."

Kunu sat with his grandfather, staring into the fire. The boy remembered the encouraging smile on his grandfather's face as he prepared to go under the boiling water. He remembered every feeling he experienced in the powerful river. He thought about their narrow escape over and over again. Grandfather was already busy making a new paddle to replace the one lost in the rapids.

Chokay broke the silence. "Kunu, you are a good grandson. You showed me your bravery. You showed me your heart. Earthmaker was with you in the water. He gave you his spirit. You did not give up. I am proud of my grandson."

"Chokay, the first time I pushed off the boat did not move. Why did it move the second time?" asked the boy.

"We did not push together the first time. I pushed before you were ready. The second time we were together. It took both of us to defeat the mighty river. We did it together."

Chokay had talked many times about people helping each other. He often told tales about the great things people were able to do when they worked together. Today Kunu understood what working together really meant.

15

A Dream Comes True

In the days ahead, the river seemed more peaceful. During the journey between Omaha and St. Joseph, Chokay remembered the river well. When he was not sure of what lay ahead, he would pull into shore to take a look downstream. They saw more and more people on the lower part of the Missouri. Omaha was a busy place, since many prospectors stopped there on their way to find gold. No one paid any attention to a boy and an old man in a tiny dugout. Kunu and Chokay were happy about that.

St. Joseph, Missouri, reminded the travelers of their ride in the awful cattle car. They remembered the suffering and death. Now they would put that all behind them. They were headed home.

Chokay was always looking for food. The deer meat was gone. Their berries and roots were gone. One evening near present-day Kansas City, the two travelers camped in a wooded area near a creek. It was October. Next to the woods was a cornfield. Most of the corn had been picked, and dead stalks stood here and there across the field.

"Kunu, go to the cornfield. Our food is almost gone. Look for corn. The farmer has finished his picking. Any that you find will be food for us."

Kunu found corn and even a few squash. He came back with his shirt loaded with the vegetables. Chokay was pleased with the boy's work. The corn had some worms in it, but it would still taste good. Grandfather had prepared some hot coals at the bottom of a hole he had dug. Kunu went to the creek and soaked the corn in the water with the husks still on each ear. Chokay covered the coals with some corn and then filled the hole with dirt and sod. Two hours later, Grandfather dug it all up. The baked corn was delicious!

Before Chokay went to sleep at night, he had Kunu help him make an even bigger hole. He filled the bottom with more hot coals. The squash and the rest of the corn was laid on a bed of grass that covered the coals. All of this was covered with dirt and sod. That night Chokay and Kunu slept well.

Grandfather was already up when Kunu awoke the next morning. The boy was shivering. It was a frosty morning. Chokay called Kunu to come and help dig the corn and squash out of the hole. The coals were still warm. The food was baked perfectly, so this breakfast was delicious. There was also a good supply of food to store in the dugout for the days ahead.

The tiny dugout passed the place where the Kansas River comes into the Missouri. Now the Missouri River turned due east to cross the state of Missouri. Some Civil War battles were being fought in this state. Chokay and Kunu avoided any contact with people wherever they saw them.

The trouble they had was always a surprise. One day a strong wind made waves so high that water came over the sides of the small boat. The wind was so powerful that tons of sand blew through the air. Chokay headed the dugout into the waves and made for shore. Another time a sudden hailstorm pelted the two paddlers with large pieces of ice. Next, a wet snow made a whole day damp, cold, and miserable. Still the two determined travelers kept going.

In many areas the river widened and became shallow. Very little rain had fallen that summer and fall. The water was low. No steamboats could travel farther up the river than the present-day Kansas City area. The water was so low in places that Kunu had to get out often to pull the boat off the sand.

The river twisted and turned. It seemed to Kunu that he had been paddling all his life. Chokay made sure the corn and squash lasted as long as possible. Only a small amount was eaten each day. Often Grandfather talked about the time they would be safely home. Every evening Chokay would tell Kunu that they were one day closer.

Kunu thought about the word *home*. Where would home be? How would they ever get past all those people who drove them from their homes? How can we hide from so many who hate us? No tree will be able to hide us that long. If we get home, how will Mother and Father find us? How will they get back? It was all more than Kunu could figure out. The boy knew he would just have to trust his grandfather. Chokay would find a way.

Due west of St. Louis, the Missouri River curves north. One day, near St. Charles, Missouri, a steamboat lay tied to a dock. Many wealthy people and their families were on the last part of their journey back to St. Louis. They had walked to a place near the river for a picnic.

As Chokay and Kunu rounded a bend in the river, they saw the people. Some of their children were playing on the riverbank. The steamboat's cooks had prepared a delicious meal under the trees. A bell was rung, calling everyone to the picnic lunch. The children left the riverbank and ran to the tables covered with wonderful food.

Chokay had already turned the dugout toward the far side of the river. When the bell rang, Kunu turned to watch the children run, but Chokay called to him excitedly. "Paddle, Kunu! These people could cause trouble. We must not take a chance."

Kunu turned and dipped his paddle in and paddled hard. The boy was not sure why, but something caused him to take one more look back. Maybe it was because he was so hungry. Maybe he wondered what it would be like to eat from a table full of so much fresh food.

After that one look, Kunu's eyes could not leave the scene. It all happened so fast. In their excitement the older children did not notice that one tiny girl stayed by the river. Kunu saw that she was making her way toward the end of a short dock that stuck out into the river.

"Chokay, look! A tiny girl is in danger. She is going to fall into the river." The boy said this as if he was sure it was going to happen. But how could he know for sure? Grandfather turned the dugout around with two powerful strokes. Somehow Chokay was sure, too. Both paddlers dug in and paddled toward the dock.

Unaware of any danger, the toddler walked closer and closer to the end of the dock. The little one stopped twice, but each time she started forward again. The tiny

girl looked like a doll as she tumbled off the end of the dock. Instantly she disappeared from sight. Ten feet past the dock her blond hair came to the surface. Then the current carried her out of sight again.

"Paddle, Kunu!" shouted Chokay. "Paddle hard!"

The boy's arms had become stronger on this long journey. Now he dug his paddle deeper than ever and pulled back on it with all his strength. The dugout moved as fast as any two people could paddle it. As the paddlers passed in front of the dock, a woman came running toward the river.

"Sarah! Sarah! Where are you?" the worried woman shouted. Sarah's mother got to the river's edge in time to see her tiny daughter go under for what might be the last time. She screamed and screamed in despair.

Kunu watched the little girl go underwater. The dugout was close to the spot. With one leap the boy was in the water. He went in right next to the place he had last seen Sarah. Suddenly his left arm struck the girl on the shoulder. Kunu grabbed her and raised her to the surface so she could breathe. The boy could not move. It was all he could do to keep his own head above the water.

"A snag! Chokay, I'm caught!" Kunu shouted.

The current was tearing at the boy, threatening to drag him under with his precious load. Chokay dropped his paddle into the dugout and leaned over the side as far as he could. As the dugout passed Kunu, Chokay clutched Sarah by the arm with his right hand. With his left hand he pulled Kunu out of the snag that had trapped him. The boy let the dugout move into quieter water before he climbed back in.

Chokay had placed Sarah on the pack and was paddling for shore. The mother's screams brought the other people to the river. All watched Kunu and Chokay paddle to shore. The boy jumped from the dugout, held on to it, and watched his grandfather leap onto shore with Sarah in his arms. The toddler was gagging on the muddy water she had swallowed. Weeds were tangled in her hair. Her dress was torn, and her shoes were gone. But she was still alive!

Chokay handed the child to her frantic mother. The crowd gathered around. One man pushed his way through to the mother's side in response to her pleas.

"Oh, doctor! Help my baby! Don't let her die!"

Without a word the doctor carefully laid the child on her stomach. He bent down and cleared the mud and weeds from her mouth and straightened her tongue. With strong but gentle hands he pressed on the child's back just below her shoulders. Sarah had not been in the water very long. In less than five minutes the girl was coughing and crying.

"Sarah will be fine, Mrs. Brown," the doctor told her. "Right now she is very frightened. And we need to take her to the steamboat to get warm and dry." Sarah's mother was unable to speak. She was sobbing too hard as she held Sarah close to her and turned to run to the steamboat.

Kunu and Chokay had watched from a distance. As soon as they saw the child would be all right, they turned to leave. But Kunu suddenly dropped to one knee. He discovered blood running from under his pant leg. There was a bad cut above his knee. It had happened when the boy landed in the snag next to Sarah.

At the same time a man called out to Chokay and Kunu. "Wait! Don't leave! You have saved our baby. Who are you?"

Chokay was kneeling next to Kunu and examining his cut when the man walked up. What will Grandfather say? Kunu wondered. What will we do now?

"We are a grandfather and a grandson traveling to our home. We go in peace."

The white man had more questions. "You are traveling in a dugout? Where is your home? How far have you traveled? Perhaps we can help you. Come, share our food. Tell us about your journey. We owe you so much. Our little Sarah is alive because you saved her life. Please stay. Eat with us. Tell us your story."

The events that followed were like a dream. None of it seemed real. They learned that Sarah's father was a wealthy landowner and cattleman who lived with his family in St. Louis. The man said he had business contacts all over the west. He insisted that Kunu and Chokay spend the night on the steamboat. Around the fireplace that night, all the people on board listened to Chokay's story. Grandfather told them everything, starting with the Sioux uprising. Kunu sat next to Chokay. The doctor had cleaned and bandaged his leg. His stomach was full. His eyes and ears took in every detail of this strange story-telling session. The boy thought it must be a dream. Only a short time ago he was in the dugout on the river. What was happening now was unbelievable.

The white people sat listening to Chokay's every word. His story seemed amazing to them. Here sat an old Winnebago man in a beautiful ballroom, surrounded by friendly white faces. Every eye was glued on Kunu's grandfather. Chokay's words flowed—as steady and powerful as the Missouri River itself. No one doubted the truth of Grandfather's words.

When Chokay had finished, Sarah's father spoke. "My friends, before this day I believed there were no good Indians anywhere in this world. I was wrong. You will be my friends forever. I want to help you with your journey. Here is my private secretary, John Morton. He will go with you by steamboat to Mankato and will help you find Karl's uncle. I will give you money to help you get settled in Minnesota. I'm sure Karl's uncle will be able to keep anyone from causing you any trouble. I will do whatever is necessary to help you. Thank you again for saving the little one whom we love so much."

So that's how we'll get home, thought Kunu. The question that had bothered him for so long had an answer that no one would ever have dreamed possible. A boy and his grandfather together had made their dream come true. Together they had endured hatred, hunger, danger, cold, storms, and everything that stood in the way of their freedom and happiness. But they didn't just endure. No, they overcame each barrier together. The story of the Winnebago people in the 1860s is one of great suffering, overcome by many such examples of their courage and determination.

Epilogue

Kunu and Chokay's steamboat trip from St. Charles, Missouri, to Mankato, Minnesota, was nothing like their steamboat-and-train travels the year before. Good food, their own room, and freedom from fear made this return trip a real luxury.

Back in Minnesota, the boy and his grandfather were welcomed by Karl's uncle. He was trying to run both his own farm and Karl's parents' place. With the Civil War still being fought, farm help was impossible to find. Karl's uncle asked Chokay and Kunu to move into the farmhouse near Milford that had stood vacant since the uprising. He paid them a fair wage to work the land and also gave them twenty acres of their own.

In 1865 the Civil War ended. Kunu's father took a steamboat to the Omaha Indian Reservation in Nebraska. There he found his wife and little girls. They had arrived safely with hundreds of other Winnebago people one month after Kunu and his grandfather had made their escape. When Kunu's father made sure his family was safe there, he set out to find Kunu and Chokay.

Enough people had heard of the pair's adventure that Kunu's father was led to Milford, Minnesota. One sunny day Kunu saw a familiar figure walking down the lane toward the farmhouse. The boy dashed down the lane at top speed and into his father's arms. Chokay came behind his grandson to welcome his own son home. Chokay's words, spoken over two years before, had foretold the coming of this moment. It was a reunion of hope and love.

The final step in the long journey came when Kunu's mother and sisters walked down the same farm road, bringing the whole family together again. This time it would be for good. Oh, yes, Wakee came running down that lane ahead of everyone—jumping, barking, and wagging his tail a mile a minute.

The record shows that not all whites in that time and place were full of hate toward the Indians. Some did help the Winnebago people during this awful time in our history. The record also shows that our land was still full of prejudice and discrimination against the Native Americans. Even today, over a hundred years later, there is too much. Chokay's words can still be used to measure the worth of any person: "Kunu, every man you meet will show you his heart and you will know if he is good or bad."

Not many Winnebago people found happy endings waiting for them after Crow Creek. Only about 1,350 of the nearly 2,000 survived the long ordeal. Most of those who escaped found themselves without a home of their own. Years later the United States government would give them a small reservation in Nebraska on the Missouri River. Those living in Minnesota and Wisconsin would eventually also receive official recognition.